TEXTILE

ORLY CASTEL-BLOOM

**THE
FEMINIST PRESS**
AT THE CITY UNIVERSITY
OF NEW YORK
NEW YORK CITY

The Reuben/Rifkin
Jewish Women Writers Series
A joint project of the Hadassah-Brandeis Institute
and the Feminist Press

Series editors: Elaine Reuben,
Shulamit Reinharz, Gloria Jacobs

The Reuben/Rifkin Jewish Women Writers Series, established in 2006 by Elaine Reuben, honors her parents, Albert G. and Sara I. Reuben. It remembers her grandparents, Susie Green and Harry Reuben, Bessie Goldberg and David Rifkin, known to their parents by Yiddish names, and recalls family on several continents, many of whose names and particular stories are now lost. Literary works in this series, embodying and connecting varieties of Jewish experiences, will speak for them, as well, in the years to come.

Founded in 1997, the Hadassah-Brandeis Institute (HBI), whose generous grants also sponsor this series, develops fresh ways of thinking about Jews and gender worldwide by producing and promoting scholarly research and artistic projects. Brandeis professors Shulamit Reinharz and Sylvia Barack Fishman are the founding director and codirector, respectively, of HBI.

OTHER BOOKS IN THE
REUBEN/RIFKIN SERIES

Published in 2013 by the Feminist Press
at the City University of New York
The Graduate Center
365 Fifth Avenue, Suite 5406
New York, NY 10016

feministpress.org

Originally published in Hebrew as *Textile* by Hakibbutz Hameuchad/Siman
Kriah in 2006 in Tel Aviv, Israel. Translated from the Hebrew by Dalya Bilu.

*This book was made possible thanks to a grant from New York State
Council on the Arts with the support of Governor Andrew Cuomo
and the New York State Legislature.*

First printing July 2013

Cover design by Faith Hutchinson
Text design by Drew Stevens

Library of Congress Cataloging-in-Publication Data
Castel-Bloom, Orly, 1960–
[Tekstil. English]
Textile / Orly Castel-Bloom ; translated by Dalya Bilu.
  pages cm
ISBN 978-1-55861-826-8
I. Bilu, Dalya, translator. II. Title.
PJ5054.C37T4513 2013
892.4'36—dc23

                                    2013004429

The Law of Shatnetz:
You shall keep my statutes . . .
You shall not sow your field
with two kinds of seed,
nor shall you wear a garment of cloth
made of two kinds of material.

Leviticus 19:19

The laws of shatnez are considered so important that one who sees another person wearing shatnez is supposed to strip the offending garment from the wearer, even in public and even if the wearer is one's rabbi. Some legal authorities, however, softened this stipulation, saying that if the person wearing shatnez is doing so unintentionally then one should wait to speak to this person privately (Shulhan Arukh 303:1 and comment of Moshe Isserles). http://www.myjewishlearning.com/practices/Ethics/Our_Bodies/Clothing/Shatnez.shtml

PART I

1

A TAXI STOOD ON THE CORNER OF YOCHEVED BAT-MIRIAM and Alexander Penn Street with its lights on and its engine off. On the back window was a message in big, white handwritten letters which said: I DRIVE ON GAS, NOT GASOLINE. AND YOU?

The light from the decorative street lamps joined the soft beams shining from amid the vegetation of the flourishing front gardens, which were all the same: three lemon cypresses, another three or five Thai ficuses, and one strange and unfamiliar tree that had shed its leaves and whose trunk was covered by thick, short thorny growths with hard, menacing points.

Taller and more prominent than these plants was a kind of slender palm whose large, feathery fronds looked as if they were bursting from a fountain with a low-pressure jet. This palm—which had been imported at the end of the nineties, was called a coconut palm (*Syagrus romanzoffiania*) even though it bore no relation to the edible coconut fruit— required very little water, while its rapid and imperious growth produced results of a cunning and historically helpful nature: it gave rise to the impression that the suburb of Tel Baruch North had not been established yesterday or the day before, but had been there for years. As the tall, flourishing coconut palms proved.

The suburb of Tel Baruch North was special, very different from the undistinguished sister suburbs surrounding it, and although it had been set up in the blink of an eye and was completely new—it proclaimed seniority and permanence, even if life itself was fleeting. An impressive achievement that explained the high price of the apartments.

GEOGRAPHICALLY SPEAKING, Tel Baruch North is situated to the north of the old Tel Baruch, but also to the south of the old established Kiryat Shaul, famous for its two vast cemeteries: one for the fallen in the wars of Israel, and the other for the ordinary dead, who are hardly ever buried there at public expense anymore, since it is over capacity and plots are hard to come by and cost a fortune.

Despite its proximity to Kiryat Shaul, it never occurred to any of the planners of the suburb, which arose as if overnight, to call the new suburb Kiryat Shaul South. And rightly so. The word "south" gives rise to horror among the many denizens, or would-be denizens, of the affluent "north," and to call a North Tel Aviv suburb Kiryat Shaul South would mean financial suicide as well as being socially insensitive. But the founders of Tel Baruch North (Telba-N.) were no fools. They drilled to the depths of human thought and took into account both the differences between North and South, and the difference between *tel*, a hill or permanent natural phenomenon, and *kirya*, a man-made township, here today and gone tomorrow. In this successful concept they cunningly encompassed death, deterioration, and extinction—in other words the absence of the above. They wanted and got a superior

location that proclaimed: I'm here to stay, and soon a generation will arise that will have no idea that once I never existed.

BUT ALL THE MOCKERY in the world vis-à-vis this expensive
piece of real estate fades and dies in the twilight hour, when a
natural pink lights up the neighborhood and all the artificial
forms of lighting that illuminate the houses are refracted by
the pale, shiny marble surfaces. Then a kind of halo is cre-
ated around some of the buildings. A halo that even lends a
spiritual significance to these stepped buildings containing
apartments with alternating porches, which provide privacy
and a certain kind of beauty, duplexes, triplexes, penthouses,
and also ordinary four-roomed apartments, which no doubt
lack for nothing either.

In those days in Israel it was no simple matter to work
up enthusiasm about anything, but the place left a powerful
impression, and gave rise, even in the driest and most arid
hearts, to eager aspirations that had seemed lost to them.
Fearful souls too, and those whose brains had been riddled
by time until they were almost hollow, could not help but be
captivated by the cute electric blinds, the graceful porches
bounded by balustrades of transparent, tempered glass. And
all these wretched, ravaged souls could not help but connect
all this beauty and luxury to some kind of posterity beyond
their grasp.

And if the blinds and the lighting and the porches themselves failed to impress, the job was done by the hanging
gardens that embellished the porches and, with unparalleled
aesthetic integrity, maintained stylistic uniformity with the
vegetation in the front gardens.

TO BE FAIR, we should point out that together with profound admiration and appreciation, it sometimes happened that envy raised its head and overcame even those who regarded themselves as cool customers, capable of exerting absolute control over the most extreme situations. This envy was fierce and devastating, and it wreaked havoc even among all kinds of social democrats, who would, on principle, never live in a place where money was so important. Like autumn leaves, the mask of hypocrisy fell from the faces of the envy stricken, their jaws dropped, and they were overcome by bitterness at the fact that they had no part in this real-estate marvel.

THE DRIVER OF THE TAXI that drove only on gas was a young man of thirty-five who had a beard and wore a black skullcap. In the past he had been a star footballer, playing center forward for Maccabi Tel Aviv, but he had become religious and retired from the game. He was waiting next to his car for a fare who had asked for a taxi that drove on natural gas, and he was wondering whether to call the fare on the phone or to wait a few minutes longer. He was the one who had arrived early after all.

The ex-football player looked around at more of the fine buildings in this new suburb that had grown up south of Kiryat Shaul, in order to take in the place that the top 10 percent had recently built for itself, in spite of the recession.

He thought that the people who lived here lived exactly like he himself would live if only he had persevered in his brilliant football career. He too felt that he was being invaded by envy, but since he was a man inspired by the wisdom of thousands of years, he succeeded in restraining his covetousness in a second.

He simply raised his eyes to heaven, just as the rabbi had told him to do at least once a day in order to understand the place of the individual as opposed to the rest of the world, took a couple of deep breaths, and erected a barrier between himself and the eternal bliss, imaginary or not, radiated by the suburb of Tel Baruch North.

IRAD GRUBER, who was only fifty, but who in the past month had been so depressed that he looked like sixty-five, walked down the path between the seasonal flower beds and looked round irritably for the taxi that was supposed to take him to the airport. With one hand he dragged a medium-sized suitcase on wheels, and in the other he held a heavy briefcase containing important documents and a laptop computer.

The driver, who Gruber immediately recognized as the famous ex-football player, opened the trunk, and only when he, the fare, came right up to him, deigned to relieve him of his suitcase and heavy briefcase.

Khhhh . . . Irad Gruber snorted in contempt, for in the many countries he had visited porters and drivers came running to take his luggage, including those who did not know who he was.

If Irad Gruber had been in a mood suited to his character, there is no doubt that he would have given the insolent driver a piece of his mind. However in recent times, as a result of other troubles, the gifted scientist had been suffering from dejection and gloom, and he therefore let the matter of the driver's insolence drop and resumed his contemplation of the world with the glum expression, full of sorrow and anguish, of someone who had recently suffered a shock.

He sat down on the backseat, his long woolen coat folded

on his knees, and set out on his ten-day trip to the most powerful country in the world. He cast a glance, empty of content, in the direction of Mikado, the commercial center of the neighborhood, and quickly averted his eyes from the white florescent light that jarred his pupils.

All that remained for him was to hope that the decision makers in the Defense Ministry and the Weapons and Infrastructure Development Administration (WIDA) had not decided to save money at the expense of his comfort, but had taken the trouble to buy him a business-class ticket, as a person of his stature deserved.

In less than a minute the ex-football star and the gifted inventor and recipient of the Israel Prize were on the Ayalon Highway, and the car that did not pollute the planet joined the traffic on the road leading to Ben-Gurion Airport.

A FEW HOURS AFTER his departure, Amanda Gruber, the wife of Irad Gruber, left the triplex on the corner of Yocheved Bat-Miriam and Alexander Penn Street, Tel Baruch North, and drove in her maroon Buick to the Medical Frontline offices in the new branch of Sea and Sun, in order to undergo a far-from-simple surgical procedure at the hands of the number two surgeon in the world in the field of intrusive cosmetic corrections, an ex-Israeli by the name of Carmi Yagoda.

From Dresden, Germany, Dr. Yagoda had been urgently summoned to perform shoulder blade implants, an operation which had become very popular with women of means in whom the years had eroded the projection of the shoulder blades, making their backs flat and boring, both in motion and at rest.

Carmi Yagoda was famous worldwide due to his success

14

in operating on the faces of children in the third world who had been born deformed, and his home in Dresden displayed impressive before-and-after photographs. In recent years he had tired of improving deformed faces, which could never be brought to perfection, and he had gone in for major plastic surgeries such as the present case. He had been particularly successful in liposuction of the waist, and in shoulder blade implants.

Yagoda was known for his precise and rapid attachment of prosthetic shoulder blades to the collarbone and the tendons and muscles that moved the shoulder blades (scapula), such as the trapezius muscle, and the muscles straightening the back and bringing the shoulder blades closer.

The ex-Israeli doctor's fine-motor skills also saved his patients from postoperative limitations on their movement. He promised Mandy that she would be able to resume swimming within a month.

MANDY'S HUSBAND knew nothing about his wife's planned hospitalization in Medical Frontline, and she saw no point in telling him, since he was absorbed in himself and his own affairs, and recently, because of problems and hitches in his present project, he couldn't see an inch in front of himself. In fact, his wife had counted on her husband's problems at work to get him out of the way. With tense apprehension she followed the news about the threatened general strike, hoping that it would break out after he left the country, and spread to El Al and the airport workers, so that he would be stuck in America for at least two or three weeks, and by the time he returned she would be completely recovered and perhaps she wouldn't even have to tell him about the operation.

A YEAR HAD PASSED since the Grubers' son Dael had joined the army and become a sniper in the Givati Brigade. It was Aya Ben-Yaish, Dael's girlfriend, who had informed Mandy where her son was serving. Ever since then Mandy had preferred to be unconscious, or semiconscious, in order not to know what was happening and not to worry uselessly about her combat soldier son.

Since she was a healthy woman, she went in and out of cosmetic surgeries. She had already undergone seven such operations, most of them on her face. Excluding the nose job she had had as a girl. To her satisfaction, her face grew to resemble that of a horse less and less from operation to operation.

The operation for which Dr. Yagoda had been flown to Israel was her eighth.

OF ALL THE WORKERS at the family pajama factory Nighty-Night, which sold most of its stock to the ultra-Orthodox population and was situated in the industrial zone in East Netanya, only Carmela Levy, Mandy's secretary and the forewoman of the sewing shop, knew the other, deeper reason for the wave of operations undergone by the boss. Only poor Carmela, whose son Yehuda Levy had been killed in Lebanon, knew that it was all for the sake of the general anesthetic during the surgery and the distracting recovery in its wake.

During the last inventory two months earlier, Mandy had told her explicitly, "If they put my son on the front lines as a sniper without asking my opinion, then I can't take the suspense. I want to sleep and sleep and wake up younger and younger the day after he gets out of the army. At his welcome home party I'll look like a woman of thirty-five," joked

Amanda, who was already breast lifted, stomach flattened, cellulite emptied in the thighs, eyebrow raised, cheekbone implanted, and raised to half-mast in the face and neck. Only her long hair remained white. Beautiful, abundant, wavy, and white, since she was allergic to every kind of hair dye. The combination of her made-over face, with the cute little nose that dated from the Passover vacation when she was seventeen, and her wavy white hair turned the woman into a walking work of art. All the more so since she took care to dress in ensembles, which Carmela considered the height of good taste, consisting of the colors white, cream, black, and greenish gray.

Carmela loved Mandy with all her heart and soul, and Mandy too did not keep her at a distance but made her into her confidante in everything concerning the pajama factory. Carmela would never forget Mandy's solicitude during the mourning period for her late Yehuda, coming every day for the shivah, crying with her, and making several large purchases at the supermarket for the many condolence callers, at her own expense. Carmela would always remember how she rose to the occasion during those terrible days.

Dael was only a child then, but Mandy had already begun to plan how she herself would endure the difficult days ahead.

Because of Carmela's loyalty, and also because of her profound knowledge of the mysteries of textiles, so necessary for a pajama factory, Mandy had said to her on a number of occasions, "You're the flower of Nighty-Night. You're my only worker with a twinkle in her eye."

Carmela's association with Nighty-Night dated from the days when Amanda's mother, Audrey Greenholtz, managed the factory. At first she would come to the plant once every few weeks, on behalf of Singer sewing machines, to oil the machines and clean them with special cloths.

After Audrey's death, Mandy promoted her. She sent her to a Labor Ministry sewing course, went on paying her salary for all three months of the course, and gave her a profession. Carmela was sure that but for Mandy, she would have come to a very bad end, as a body cast up by the sea onto the Netanya beach.

After the boy's shivah, Carmela lost the will to live. Mandy couldn't stand to see it happening, and she sent her to a great psychiatrist who in two months got her out of bed and put her on her feet. In spite of all the differences, there was a rare, strong friendship between Mandy and Carmela, a kind of secret pact, and in Nighty-Night they said that Carmela Levy received a salary of over six thousand five hundred net, and that she got more coupons on holidays, and more rest and recreation days than anyone else.

2

TWO WEEKS BEFORE THE LATEST OPERATION, AMANDA called her grown-up daughter Lirit, and confided in her. Lirit lived on a small-holders cooperative called Brosh next to Te'ashur in the northern Negev, with her boyfriend Shlomi. The Grubers, busy with their own affairs, were relieved that their twenty-two-year-old daughter had found herself a forty-two-year-old boyfriend (although Mandy thought he was closer to fifty) and had gone to live with him in an organic paradise in the Negev, far from their eyes. Every month they would throw a few thousand into her bank account for her to do with as she pleased.

As far as Mandy was concerned, Lirit's future was too uncertain and her choice of partners too haphazard, lacking in planning and content. At the end of her NCO-Casualties course she had fallen in love with a Jamaican Rastaman called Lucas, whom she met at a Reggae club in town.

For almost two years, during her entire army service, Lirit went about with this Lucas, until three months before her discharge from the IDF Mandy invited him for a heart-to-heart in a park on King George Street. She offered him twenty thousand dollars cash to break off relations with her daughter and leave the country never to return. He agreed, and one week later he vanished, leaving a letter, or more precisely a note, in which he wrote in Hebrew with Latin letters: It's better this way. Sorry.

Lirit's heart was broken by Lucas's abandonment, and she either cried all day or didn't speak. Because of the nature of her work in the army, the psychiatrist gave her a month of excused duty days, to recover her balance.

Even after she got over her depression and returned to her terrible task as an NCO-Casualties, this confused young soul agonized over the question: Why so suddenly? How come she hadn't noticed any warning signs of the fading of the Jamaican's love? Why did he disappear from one day to the next?

Something in her ability to comprehend her fellow man was fundamentally flawed, she concluded.

And from then on Lirit got it into her head that anyone who attached himself to her was doing so out of pity or karmic repair, with no hint on the horizon of how she would disabuse herself of this mistaken idea.

After the army Lirit went to the kibbutz seminar to learn how to be a nursery school teacher, because the company of innocent little children who didn't yet know what was waiting for them, made her feel good. She made them laugh and fascinated them by making all kinds of faces and noises, and her teachers told her that she had what it takes.

SHLOMI WAS FAR LESS PROBLEMATIC than Lucas, even though this esoteric departure from the norm was also a far cry from what Amanda had in mind. She couldn't understand why her daughter couldn't find someone cute (and there were plenty of cute guys around today), of her own age and religion, preferably from Israel, preferably in Israel, preferably from the center of the country and from a satisfactory family—and she wished Lirit would study something (even if it was only teaching nursery school) and marry him. Mandy thought that if Lirit got married she wouldn't have to worry about her anymore. She thought of someone along the lines of a promising student of business administration, or even a young math teacher who wasn't a pedophile.

She was afraid that her daughter would repeat the mistake that she herself had made when she married Irad Gruber. Although it was true that in his youth he had been great looking, a real charmer with a full head of hair, not like today with his receding hairline, but as a kibbutz leaver he suffered from a lack of earning ability. She had spent a fortune on financing his doctorates and living expenses for the duration. In the course of the years he had progressed and traveled the world, while she stayed stuck with the 100 percent cotton pajamas with no fear of religiously prohibited impurities.

And even after he had completed all his degrees in biology, technology, and engineering, as well as postgraduate courses in personnel management and administration, Irad Gruber remained a financial burden on his wife. Without funding from any outside agency he applied himself to all kinds of inventions in every possible field, conveying to all and sundry the sense that he was about to make an important breakthrough.

"It's hard to support a genius," she would joke, without raising a laugh from anyone, including herself.

AND INDEED, after a not insignificant number of years the spiral escalators invented and designed by Irad Gruber gained worldwide recognition and distribution, and the

Ministry of Culture, Science, and Sport (CSAS) intervened and provided funding, and Gruber gave Israel's reputation a boost at a terrible time, when most of the world disapproved of its policies. Many air-raid shelters throughout the world acquired the spiral escalators, as did airports and shopping malls. Much space was saved by this Israeli with his brilliant invention, which in certain places prevented the chopping down of forests or other environmental destruction.

He made many millions for the state, and a few for himself. Mandy fell on the money and invested it in profitable ventures. Gruber was disdainful and didn't object. Money wasn't his field, he liked to say.

On the fifty-fourth anniversary of the establishment of the state, he was awarded the Israel Prize for bringing credit to the country in difficult days and injecting important foreign capital into its resources. On the fifty-fifth anniversary of the state he was granted the honor of lighting a torch at the official Independence Day celebration on Mount Herzl.

A WEEK AFTER the attack on the Twin Towers, Gruber was approached by the Weapons and Infrastructure Development Administration (WIDA) at the Defense Ministry and invited to a meeting with important people from the highest echelons. It upset them to see a local, homegrown talent wasted for the benefit of random crowds, coming and going in international airports and shopping centers, while what people desperately needed now was simply to stay alive.

He had a series of meetings at the Defense Ministry with various VIPs, and in a brief and to-the-point conversation in a cafe in the London Ministore, between the deputy defense minister and Irad Gruber, the ministry hired the services of the gifted man to design and produce special, lightweight protective suits that would not limit the movements of the people wearing them, unlike the armor worn by medieval knights, or the heavy flak jackets of our own day issued only to those on the front line.

These important suits were known by the code name "TESU," or T-suits (in other words, terror suits). The plan was to issue them to all the troops on active service and also to the reserves, and later on to supply them to the entire civilian population, in the event of a terrorist attack.

This was a formula that suited the needs of Irad Gruber down to the ground. The escalators had brought him money, a local prize, international fame and respect, and the new suits would bring him the Nobel Prize. The government provided him with all the conditions for the manufacture of the T-suits. Mandy thought that she would have to attach a catheter to her husband's head to drain off all the piss that had gone to it since he had received the Israel Prize. Otherwise it was liable to burst with self-satisfaction.

There were about sixty patents registered in Gruber's name, and he had started work on some of them before being approached by the Defense Ministry. Mandy feared the success of more grandiose projects. What he had already achieved was enough for her. But from Irad's point of view this was an opportunity to prove that he wasn't just a mercenary publicity hound, as a certain newspaper had claimed, but also a great humanist. He set all his other ideas aside, and for three years he had devoted himself exclusively to the ultimate rescue suit—the TESU.

AMANDA HAD ALWAYS raised the children alone, without any help from Irad. As soon as she recovered from the shoulder blade surgery, she planned to drop in to the Steimatzky branch in Neve Avivim and pick up a few books to prepare her spaced-out daughter for the psychometric tests. And as a girl who had grown up on lowbrow juvenile literature, she would get her a few magazines too, to look at when she was resting from her studies.

Mandy liked going to the shopping center in Neve Avivim, because she had done her shopping there for twenty years when she was living in a penthouse at 44 Tagore Street.

She usually bought the classics Dael asked her to get for him there too, although she sometimes ordered them for him on the Internet. She had heard, from Aya Ben-Yaish again, that immediately after a targeted assassination her Dael was left with the smell of gunpowder on his hands, never mind how often he washed them and what soap he used, and only immersion in very high literature distracted him from the smell.

The child therefore took advantage of the long lulls between ambushes and liquidations in order to read the classic of world literature: Stendhal, *Madame Bovary*, *Don Quixote*, Thomas Mann, Turgeniev, Tolstoy, *Crime and Punishment*, Kafka, and so on. He didn't ignore the classics of Hebrew literature either, and was particularly fond of Mendele Mocher Seforim and all kinds of old books with titles that began with the words "The Collected Works of . . ." He also had a notebook that was very precious to him, in which he wrote down Hebrew words that were unfamiliar to him because they were no longer in use, and on weekends, after surfing his favorite porno sites, he would translate them into contemporary Hebrew and enter the site of the Language Academy to offer his suggestions.

He had developed a method of reading in breadth, in other words he would read a number of books at once. Breadth reading demanded a special effort and distracted him from current affairs. He would also test himself to see that he wasn't getting mixed up between the plots of the novels and putting a character from one book into another book by mistake. These tests were also excellent etudes for the mind, enabling him to maintain thinking in breadth as opposed to his linear thinking as a sniper, and he thought that in this way he saved himself, because when all was said and done Dael was a very sensitive boy.

Mandy didn't know that her son read several books at once, sometimes as many as five, and nevertheless she correctly interpreted his intensive reading as an act of *balance*. After shooting someone, he felt the need to connect with something uplifting, and she was very willing to respond to this noble need.

A FEW MINUTES BEFORE the important conversation, two weeks before the surgery, Mandy sat in her car in the car wash and prepared herself. Soap from thin boring pipes sprayed the car, and giant brushes emerged from hiding and scrubbed energetically, until the dark red car was completely covered with a thick layer of white foam.

Inside the foam, from which she was protected by the car, Mandy wondered what would be the most effective way of appealing to her daughter to make her agree to leave Shlomi in the Negev, and their natural farm based on a number of "ideals" she couldn't remember at the moment, and take on the burden of being Mandy Gruber for ten, maximum twelve, days.

The mother aimed herself at a balance between forcefulness and tenderness, and got ready for the very possible contingency in which Lirit would begin to yell and go berserk. In this case, she would cut off the conversation and call again later. That was the advantage of these cell phones, which sometimes disconnected.

On the other end of the line, long rings repeated themselves without a human or nonhuman response. They must be digging up the beets, thought Mandy.

The car had emerged from the tunnel shining and beautiful since she had had it waxed. She waited at the stop sign before the right turn, without noticing that the road was empty and she could go. She was busy listening to the long dial tones somewhere in the Negev.

Finally Lirit answered.

"What did I take you away from?"

"Shlomi wanted me to come and see something."

"What?" She turned right as if there was a traffic light there and it had just changed to green.

"What?"Lirit was surprised at the interest.

"Yes, what?"

"That tree bark prevents weeds from growing, and there's no need to spray anything. We're going to collect tree bark in a minute."

"I understand, enjoy yourselves," said Mandy, and added, "Darling."

Lirit was sure that her mother was encouraging her in her way of life, and she was surprised and happy, but a second later she realized that it was only the preamble to a serious request.

Mandy told Lirit that *this time too* she would have to come up north during her hospitalization in order to stand in for her. In other words, as she was well aware, this wasn't the first time that she had had to stand in for her. Both in her previous home and in this one Mandy had called on her. It couldn't be helped. It was an emergency. She should see it as a war. She would have to sleep in the luxurious triplex in Tel Baruch North, and not in the ruin where she was living now. To disconnect and activate the alarm system, to keep an eye on the Columbian so she wouldn't steal her cosmetics, like the one before her and the Filipina before that, who had made long distance calls to all her friends in Manila. To arrange for the Columbian to get the key and return it. And above all: to take herself every day to the family pajama factory in Netanya and manage it to the extent that Lirit was capable of managing anything.

She asked her first-born to make an effort on her behalf, because this time she really needed this operation. Carmela would help Lirit with whatever she required. "It's all arranged, my sweet. He'll manage without you for a few days. Sometimes it's healthy to take a break," she hurried to soften the impression.

"I can't believe that you're actually going through with this insane operation," said Lirit.

"What's insane about it?" asked Mandy and passed the turnoff to Tel Baruch North by mistake. "My shoulder blades have become eroded, and I'm having replacements implanted. They've already done three thousand of them to date. I'm not prepared to look at my back and see sunken skin where my exquisite shoulder blades once were."

At this moment Shlomi came in and lay down on the sofa without doing anything. Lirit's mother went on talking to her, she said that she had only left her a few little tasks that she could take care of easily, but Lirit's attention had already been distracted. Negative vibrations were reaching her from the tired man with the slow movements who was lying on the sofa. Altogether, he had been giving off a lot of negative energy recently, and sometimes it seemed to her that he was aiming it straight at her, because she had forgotten to water their organic vegetable garden a few times and things had died. In addition to which, the carrots had failed, the cucumbers had holes in them, and the pumpkin had rotted.

Lately he hardly spoke to her, as opposed to periods when he even talked too much. And she, who suffered from severe attention deficit and hyperactivity disorder (ADHD), was unable to listen to such long speeches of at least an hour against globalization and destruction and the exploitation of Africa and the children in Southeast Asia. The communication between these two suffered from severe limitations, since in addition to Lirit's ADHD, Shlomi's verbal skills were poor. He would sometimes begin sentences with the word "what," and the words that followed were not always in the right order, and he added unnecessary similes, and repeated them several times, and all this verbal inflorescence was supposed to be connected to the initial "what."

Lirit said "Good," and "No problem" to her mother, in order to get the conversation over. And even before she had succeeded in taking in the gist of her mother's words, before she had started to examine in theory the possible effects of leaving the farm or her relations with Shlomi, the latter rose from the sofa, took a few steps, walked past her, went outside, and called her to come and see something, this time at the bottom of the garden. The red worms had multiplied and fattened in the compost heap. She hurried over and expressed exaggerated admiration for the compost and the size of the worms, whatever it took to stop him sulking and to moderate this negativity of his.

AFTER SHE HAD EXPRESSED such enthusiasm for the work of the worms, Shlomi smiled his good smile at her and she breathed a sigh of relief. He wasn't sulking and he wasn't cross with her, he was simply absorbed in himself, as people sometimes were absorbed in themselves, he explained to her on his own initiative without her asking. She sat down on the old sofa and Shlomi went to fetch his latest photographs. One of his photographs had once been published in *The Voice of the South* for twenty-seven dollars.

Shlomi was not only an idealistic organic farmer, but also a gifted photographer, and he was trying to get into the journalism market in the south of the country. This time he dwelled only on his latest photographs, especially of the floods in the Negev, and Lirit sat on his lap and said:

"How lovely," and "That's amazing," and "This one is to die for."

"Tell me," Shlomi asked his girlfriend, and shook her off him because her embrace was a little suffocating and he felt hot, "do you think I could offer these pictures to the Gates of the Negev local council as a calendar? That means hundreds of dollars. What I've got here isn't only the floods, in other words ruin and destruction. Take a look at this one . . ." He showed her a close up of flowers. "And this one . . . and this one . . . I think we're going to have a fantastic spring this year, by the way."

"If not Gates of the Negev, then some other local council," said Lirit. "A person would have to be an idiot not to take them." She stood up, changed into her smoking clothes, and went outside, accompanying the entire process with facial grimaces that related to her conversation with her mother shortly before.

She knew that her mother wanted her, when the day came, to inherit the factory and continue the tradition, and she wasn't at all sure that she wanted to, but in the meantime no need had arisen for her to express any wish in the matter. Her mother was a strong, healthy woman. It only annoyed her that Dael showed no interest in the pajama factory, and that it was so clear to their mother that she was the one who would take command of the family concern while Dael was expected to charge ahead. The guy had already acquired a profession in the army, not like her, who in her army service had only learned how to grab hold of collapsing people a minute before their bodies hit the floor or some piece of furniture.

And indeed, Dael had organized a future for himself after the army. The day after his discharge he was going to fly straight to Hollywood and become a paparazzi to the stars. Judging by his success as a sharp shooter, the Hollywood stars were in for a big surprise. Dael thought that after he made his first fortune from his photos he would open a school right there in Los Angeles for paparazzi photographers, who would have to pass strict tests in order to be accepted, and whose year-long studies would cost them tens of thousands of dollars.

THE NIGHTY-NIGHT pajama factory had been founded by Audrey Greenholtz, Mandy's mother, in the middle of the sixties, soon after the two of them arrived in Israel from the former Rhodesia, when the child was eight.

For years Audrey held to the opinion that the factory should serve only the ultra-Orthodox population, since the ultra-Orthodox population was the most stable thing in Israel. Any deviation from this target population would spell the end of the factory, in the opinion of its founder.

Difficult life circumstances had made Audrey Greenholtz into a fighter as well as a schemer. She thought it was a mistake for mothers to be soft on their daughters, and she raised her daughter to be tough, drilling it into her that giving in wasn't an option, no matter what.

When the Rhodesian police came to the Greenholtz family home and informed the mother that the body of her husband, Aaron Greenholtz, had been found headless on the roadside, she did not collapse or start screaming, but carried on resourcefully. This resourcefulness she tried to pass on to her daughter Mandy, who tried to pass it on to her daughter Lirit, with diminishing success from generation to generation.

When Audrey died in 1989, and Mandy took charge, she put up a dummy tombstone to her father, Aaron Greenholtz, in the Kiryat Shaul cemetery, according to whose inscription his memory would never fade. But the truth was that his memory didn't exist. Mandy had forgotten him completely.

In the middle of the nineties, Mandy thought of adding

another line to her father's tombstone, something along the lines of "Murdered in race riots in Rhodesia, 19—" but she didn't do it.

AUDREY COULDN'T STAND Israel and she never stopped telling her daughter and the few friends she had here that it was only Aaron's death that had forced her to come to the Levant, and that nothing but terrible distress would have brought her to a place of no distinction, full of men with weak characters. She was enraged against Israeli men, who gave her the cold shoulder because she already had a daughter from a marriage that had ended in death, and who regarded her as irrelevant.

During her first days in Israel, Audrey acted out of character—and collapsed. She barely brought herself to acquire a three-roomed apartment in Arlozorov Street in Tel Aviv. She was told that this was classic North Tel Aviv, and that it would always remain classic.

But six months after arriving in Israel, Audrey got out of bed and she never fell again. She called in renovators, who turned right into left and ceiling into floor. During the period of the renovations the two of them stayed in the old Sheraton Hotel, which no longer exists and today there is a big hole where it used to be. Every morning she set out from the hotel to take three or four buses to Netanya, to the factory she set up there in the industrial zone.

Audrey herself invented the name Nighty-Night. Her knowledge of the Hebrew language was nothing to write home about, and she thought the name was clear enough for people in the Levant. She acquired a few classic Singer sewing machines, and insisted on handwork even when technology made faster and more efficient machines available.

Only in this way can the connection of the material with the thread be felt, while the movement of the foot accelerates the blood circulation and improves the concentration of the workers, Audrey explained her conservatism.

There was also the factory outlet that was opened before the holidays, and then—what a flood! Religious women bought pajamas in bulk and paid in cash, and the child Mandy got a kick out of being in charge of the cash register of the outlet, which also, of course, sold second-class goods for those who could not afford to buy first-class pajamas.

The adolescent Mandy was very happy when the government changed the currency and varied her life behind the cash register. She liked counting the change out loud, sometimes also in Yiddish, for the women in the wigs, and seeing the notes piling up in the compartments of the cash register made her feel really good, because she saw how happy it made her mother.

"Come and see," she called her, and her mother would call back from the distance: "Nice work!"

IN THE BEGINNING there were about a dozen seamstresses working in the factory, but today, still on Singer machines but new electric ones, there are sixty, most of them ultra-Orthodox, and others from different sectors of religious and secular Judaism. After the death of her mother, Mandy didn't change a thing in the factory, partly because she was afraid it would bring bad luck, but mainly because it was her mother's will, and she complied as usual.

Thus it happened that at the dawn of the third millennium there was a factory in Israel where people worked almost like once upon a time. From Audrey's deathbed,

Mandy was delivered another fatal blow. Instead of occupying herself with her death and parting from this world, the dying woman issued instructions as if tomorrow morning she would be opening another twenty branches of Nighty-Night. First of all, she ordered Mandy not to be tempted to change the machines. And she also forbade her to change the system of locking up the factory: eight heavy locks on the gate without any remote control. In addition she commanded her daughter not to remain alone in the event that "he," God forbid, should die before his time (she always called Irad "he," never mind how many prizes he got or how many inventions were registered in his name with the patents registrar as intellectual property). And if she ever got it into her head to divorce him, Audrey warned her, it would mean three generations of lonely women in the family, since her mother too had raised her alone, because her own father died young from typhus or malaria.

"You hear? We don't get divorced!"

Mandy almost fainted at the sound of this sudden announcement. She knew that her mother was opposed to divorce, but not for a moment could she have guessed that on her very deathbed she would slam her with an ace like this. She had planned to run to the rabbinate and open divorce proceedings as soon as the seven days of mourning were over and now after the dying woman's veto the only place she could divorce Irad was in her imagination, which she didn't have.

She sank into melancholy, and everyone around her, even Carmela, attributed her sadness to her parting from her mother.

LIFE WITH THE GENIUS Gruber became more and more difficult as the years went by, and the task of putting up with the man fell mainly on Mandy. He never listened to anyone and talked without stopping while at the same time apologizing for being a nuisance and saying that he knew he was a nuisance but he couldn't help it. It didn't depend on him. His genius mind was unable to stop inventing unique inventions that nobody had ever thought of.

Over the course of the years he stopped needing any kind of intimacy, and Mandy couldn't see an end to all this ego trip. The children had become immune in their childhood to his long speeches, which could go on for hours because he liked to think out loud, and accordingly only Mandy was left to supply him with an audience. Again and again she was forced to listen to simulations of presentations he planned to present to capitalists so they would invest in this or that invention produced by his brilliant mind, and she had to make comments even if she didn't have any and even if she sometimes stopped paying attention.

NOT LONG AFTER Dael's bar mitzvah, which was held in the Neve-Kodesh Synagogue in Neve Avivim and considered a highly successful affair, came Gruber's success with the spiral escalator, and she enjoyed a little respite from the headaches he gave her.

But the comeback arrived in the interval between the spiral escalators and the special protective suits. During this period Gruber experienced emptiness and boredom, and all that remained to entertain him was to hone in on Mandy again. Accordingly Mandy found herself spending unnecessary overtime in the factory. But then he would drive her up the wall worse than ever over the weekends, following her all over the house and telling her about his thoughts and ideas. Sometimes she would shut herself in the lavatory, but he would stand behind the door and go on talking.

His genius bordered on mysticism. In order to give expression to his many talents all he needed was a pencil and a piece of paper. "The genius with the pencil" he was called in many places, including at the Ministry of Defense. At home they had a large collection of pencils with erasers and without, for in the course of the years Gruber had developed a fear that an idea would come to him and he wouldn't have a pencil to write it down and it would escape his memory.

AFTER DAEL WAS DRAFTED into the army, Mandy began the business with the plastic surgery, and most of the time her face was bandaged. Gruber told her that she looked like the heroine in Georges Franju's movie, *Eyes Without a Face*. The father of the heroine was a sadistic surgeon who performed experiments on his daughter and ruined her face.

Obviously she couldn't show herself at the factory like this, and once more Carmela came into the picture. Every night Mandy would sneak into their garage in Tel Baruch North, start the car, and drive to Netanya, to the pajama factory. There was something inhuman about the woman with the bandaged face racing alone in the American car on Highway 4. Once the police stopped her for speeding, and the policemen were very embarrassed. Mandy told them that her face had been burned when she was making chips for the children, and the explanation satisfied them and they even let her off and only told her to be careful not to exceed the speed limit in future.

In the factory Carmela would be waiting for her with all the paperwork, and they would go over all the events of the day together. The official version given to the workers was that due to intolerable tension stemming from some mental crisis or other, the boss had developed a skin disease, which was definitely not terminal, but until further notice prohibited her from exposing herself to the sun.

How would Mandy have survived the endless operations without the boundless loyalty of Carmela, who was so kind hearted that she even released Mandy from the burden of gratitude? Day after day she simply repeated the words, "Now it's my turn. You helped me, now I'm helping you."

And every time Mandy would throw her eyes up to heaven and say:

"There's no comparison . . ."

ONCE SHE DARED to arrive at the factory with her face bandaged not at night, but at dawn. She had to approve fabrics she had ordered, with new colors and patterns, and she needed daylight in order to see the main shade of the fabric properly and to feel it. Feeling the fabric by daylight was an essential stage in its acquisition and Mandy, like her mother, was able to tell the quality of the knitting, of the warp and woof of the material, in the blink of an eye, and how it would withstand frequent laundering.

After she had approved the fabrics, she turned toward the parking lot, but before she could get there and drive rapidly away, five seamstresses arrived early for work. They didn't know whether to pretend not to see her, or to go up and ask her how she was. They didn't know what the right thing to do was in a case like this. Suddenly one of them burst out laughing, and tried in vain to stifle her laughter, because the last thing Mandy was capable of arousing in her present plight was fear. The others sniggered too. And when they disappeared from sight she heard all five of them laughing.

Two hours later, after returning to the triplex on the corner of Yocheved Bat-Miriam and Alexander Penn Streets, she sent all five notices of dismissal by SMS, and they complained about it to the labor tribunal. The case is still under review, but a photograph of the five women has already appeared in the press under the heading: "Dismissed by SMS."

Mandy wasn't bothered by the bad press. In any case, most of her customers only read the ultra-Orthodox newspaper.

3

LIRIT PREFERRED THE TRIPLEX IN TEL BARUCH NORTH TO
the penthouse in Neve Avivim. Although she never said anything out loud, because she had hardly ever had the opportunity to stay in Telba-N., it was evident that she was glad to
move there after life close to the earth and close to Shlomi.
Indirectly, therefore, her mother's plastic surgeries did her a
favor. And since this time, as it sometimes happened, Gruber
was abroad, Lirit took over her parents' handsome suite and
settled down to reflections of a futuristic nature, about how
her own apartment would look when the day came. In these
plans for her future, neither Shlomi, nor his enlarged nature
photographs decorating the walls, appeared in her mind's
eye. She lay in bed like a princess and watched her favorite
channel on the huge television facing her, the E! Channel,
reporting on the difficulties in the lives of Hollywood stars
in the past and present. She was in no hurry to get to the
factory in the mornings, she knew that Carmela was on the
job, and only when it was nearly lunch time she dropped in
to Nighty-Night to see that everything was under control. In
the meantime she saw a repeat showing of a program about
Winona Ryder, and allowed herself to drift off into different
thoughts. For example where should *she* have her children,
in a Jacuzzi or in a dolphin pool? It was clear to her that she

would go for one of these options, after hearing a videotape of some actress, not Ryder, who gave birth to her first son in a Jacuzzi, and then her first daughter in a dolphin reef.

On no account did she wish to repeat her mother's mistakes, giving birth to her and to Dael in a hospital and relying on a local anesthetic. Lirit didn't want any anesthetics, local or general. She knew that the secret of her strength was to be the antithesis of her mother.

On the other hand, the design of the new house was definitely something she could adopt. For weeks Mandy had searched for an architect to plan the interior before the contractor went for the standard. She drove to see the houses in Arsuf at the suggestion of recommended architects. She saw five possibilities in Arsuf, and three in communities where well-known people had built themselves homes. She didn't like any of them. Luckily she heard about a certain Oz Bonfil, a gifted Israeli designer who had gone to live in Tuscany and changed his name to Pasquale Bonfil. The person in question came to Israel twice a year, on Passover and Rosh Hashanah, to visit his sister. Mandy flew him over and put him up in the Dan Panorama at the end of winter, beginning of spring, and he stayed in the hotel for two months, for at a certain stage he saw fit to supervise the progress of the work himself.

Before Bonfil began work, Amanda presented him with two no-nos. One, that there be nothing in the apartment reminiscent of the Levant, nothing exotic, oriental, or Indian. And two, he was on no account to exceed the generous budget she had allowed him, because although from a socioeconomic point of view they belonged to the top 10 percent, they didn't belong to the top 1 percent and not to the top one-thousandth either. There was a difference that wasn't a nuance between the top 10 percent and the top 1 percent.

"In the top 1 percent, the sky's the limit," said Mandy, "but with us the limit is lower," and she told him the sum she had in mind.

At first Bonfil grumbled about the second veto and argued that he only worked with people for whom the sky was the limit, but afterward he agreed and said that if he had to stay within the framework she had given him, they could forget about the possibility of uniting the first and second levels in one big space, and crowning it with a ceiling that had become available from a cathedral in Bologna.

Mandy took a week to think about the possibility of bringing the ceiling from the Bolognan cathedral for the unification between the first and second levels recommended by Bonfil. Sometimes the idea seemed fine to her and sometimes it seemed silly. She took into account the cost of bringing an entire ceiling from Bologna, with the insurance and the headaches, asked herself why she should do away with a level and turn a triplex into a duplex, she could have bought a duplex to begin with, so what if the ceiling would be high and ecclesiastical? And after she had considered every aspect, and calculated the cost, she decided: No!

They decided to leave the ceilings as they were and dwell mainly on the division of the space and its design. And in the end what came out was such a charming little palace that Mandy didn't feel right hanging the old pictures from the previous house on its walls. She went around a few galleries and bought a few interesting originals. Bonfil agreed to pop over from Tuscany for a couple of days and help her find the right place for each painting, and he didn't ask a fee for his advice, and even said that it was fun.

LIRIT THOUGHT THAT what was so great about the house was that it was both as amazingly comfortable and as gorgeous as an adorable hotel in a European capital, without the artificial manners of the reception clerks.

The film about Winona Ryder came to an end and Lirit got into the Jacuzzi feeling that she had come to a certain conclusion, both as a result of her private thoughts and as a result of the film about the difficulties in the life of the Hollywood star, but in fact she hadn't come to any conclusion at all, since she hadn't actually defined her doubts to herself yet.

The Jacuzzi had not been used for quite a time and it took a while for the water to come out of the nine jets, but after a few minutes she abandoned herself to the currents massaging her muscles, and she thought, how can this compare to the miserly trickle coming out of the rusty shower in her and Shlomi's house. She was sure that if she could only succeed in getting him into the Jacuzzi—perhaps if she got in with him, after all it was a Jacuzzi for two—he wouldn't be able to deny his body this pleasure.

But she knew that after Shlomi had been shocked by their leather living room, and asked if Mandy had a fur coat, and she said she didn't know—there was no chance he would come to her parents' home any time soon, let alone take a dip in their Jacuzzi. She switched on the radio next to the foaming tub, and read the label still stuck to its side that informed her that the Jacuzzi possessed 1.2 horsepower, nine jets, a special regulator governing the strength of the massage, and underwater lighting. She looked for the regulator, and tried out all kinds of combinations, until she found the one she liked best. Strong on the upper back and shoulders.

Suddenly something bothered her. She felt guilty for being in the Jacuzzi and not at least at work, or perhaps even more worthy: by the side of her mother who was undergoing her surgery today. She was sorry she didn't have a telephone with her in the Jacuzzi, because she didn't feel like getting up, and also because she didn't know what to say if her mother asked her why she wasn't at the factory.

Still, she had gone to Medical Frontline with her yesterday. She was there all day, and it drove both of them crazy. They argued nonstop. Lirit took a lot of crap from her until she finally lost her temper and said that her stomach hurt and she was going home. And Mandy had explicitly asked her to go to the factory today, but she, Lirit, didn't have it in her *system* to be with her mother on the day of the operation, or at least in the factory from 8:00 a.m. People are sometimes mean and I can be mean sometimes too, she thought to herself and sighed. It wasn't clear yet, maybe she would still go, maybe she would still make it, although how much could a person be expected to take?

Her heart contracted, and she got out of the Jacuzzi steeped in guilt.

While she was drying her hair she remembered that yesterday, when they gave her mother an EKG, they told her she had the heart of a thirty-year-old, and how happy it made her. The cardiologist said that it wasn't a compliment but a fact. All day Mandy basked in this fact, because she always felt bad about not taking part in serious sports with an emphasis on heart-lung endurance.

"You see?" she said to Lirit, "And you nag me for not going to a gym."

"I never nagged you, I just said that physical activity would do you good. It can also dispel anxiety. Endorphins."

"Okay okay okay," Mandy dismissed her, "you know everything. About endorphins too."

Mandy had a lot of anger against Lirit in her heart, at this moment and in general. She was not satisfied with the rate of her daughter's progress in life, even though she had never asked herself: Progress to where? And to what? Except perhaps once or twice when the girl was a teenager.

After they made up, Mandy urged her daughter to go to the factory, "So things won't descend into anarchy there like in the Palestinian Authority."

"In any case I have to go in for a tête-à-tête with Dr. Carmi Yagoda," she reinforced her words.

"Can't I come with you?"

"No," commanded Mandy and went into the room, leaving Lirit to drive to the family factory.

YAGODA EXPLAINED EVERYTHING again to Mrs. Amanda Gruber from beginning to end, all the stages of the operation. Afterward he asked her to remove her blouse and bra, and to lie on her stomach and not to move. He concentrated and marked the place with Indian ink where the new shoulder blades she had chosen would be installed. And then he let her sit up and showed her, with the help of two mirrors, the sketch he had drawn. Mandy nodded her head to signify her approval, and while she was getting dressed Yagoda told her that up to recently shoulder blade surgery had been a much more complicated business, since the surgeon had to find the two original shoulder blades which had been absorbed by the back, and to return them to their rightful place, more or less symmetrically, and to sharpen the point of the shoulder blade which had been blunted by time. Many women were shocked after the operation. The new operation had been preceded by a courageous conception of surrender to the ravages of time: what was gone was gone, never to return, and therefore it was necessary to take out the used shoulder blades and replace them with new ones. The points of the shoulder blades, points, evident when the hands were moved, the patient could choose according to her taste, before the surgery was performed. Mandy had already chosen.

SHORTLY BEFORE THE OPERATION, when the nurse came to give Mandy a shot, she also asked her if she would have any objections to being photographed to advertise Medical Frontline. She was the fiftieth woman in Israel to have the operation. But Mandy refused point blank. All her life she had run away from publicity, and not because she couldn't rub shoulders with the highest in the land, if she wanted to.

She simply didn't like going anywhere with her husband, and avoided being seen with him in public. Sometimes, when both of them had to leave the house, he in the Buick and she in a taxi, she would linger over her makeup, or her eyeliner, just so they wouldn't leave the house together.

Only on rare occasions did the Grubers go as a couple to a cocktail party hosted by a colleague in the scientific field, or by some big bug in the secret service, the Mossad, or the aircraft industry. In all the years of their marriage, they went out to a restaurant together twice. Mandy detested all that "Pleased to meet you," "How well you look," "So glad you could come . . ."

It was time for the general anesthetic she was waiting for. She lay in surrender on the operating table, under the bright lights.

Everyone was dressed in green with masks on their faces, and they treated her like a child. They called her sweetheart and *meideleh*, and said *nu, nu, nu,* too, as if she was a naughty little girl. She liked this strange pampering. The operating-room nurse asked her to turn over and lie on her stomach if she didn't want her shoulder blades in front. The anesthetist said, "No no. First I put her under and then *we* turn her over."

"As you wish," said Dr. Carmi Yagoda and moved aside, and the anesthetist jabbed her. Mandy managed to turn over by herself, and then she was obliterated. The nurse put a green sheet on her back and folded it. Only the area of Mandy's upper back was left exposed, and on it the outlines of the operation that Dr. Yagoda had sketched the day before.

FLYING COACH CLASS to New York did not suit a man of Irad Gruber's position. People squeezed into their seats like chickens in a coop. Nobody had told him that there would be a two-hour layover in Paris. And all around him was a group of hyperactive fifteen-year-old boys, the sons of ex-Israelis living in Chicago, whose two counselors were unable to control them. Gruber thought it was the worst flight of his life.

Earlier, on the ground, he had tried to upgrade his ticket. He was used to flying business class and there was no reason on earth why he should accept a drop in his standard of living now. But the ground attendant at boarding told him that business class was full, that all the seats next to the emergency exits were taken, and there were no window seats left.

Gruber felt as if he was trapped in a flying cage. Rubbing shoulders with the loudmouthed masses of the people of Israel made him ill. Now he had no doubt that his status in the eyes of the Defense Minister had taken a dive, the only question was when the dive would be arrested and his body would hit the ground and they would bury him together with the whole TESU project.

The TV screen on the back of the seat in front of him showed the temperature outside and the distance from the unexpected destination city: Paris. He switched channels. Actors too young for him to know their names appeared, making the movie of no interest to him. He looked for quiet music on the audio channels, found the oldies channel, and listened to Diana Ross and Marvin Gaye singing "You are everything and everything is you."

At Charles de Gaulle Airport he got off and waited, according to instructions, in an isolated hall with cold croissants on plastic plates and a hot water urn that refused to come to a boil.

When the call to return to the plane came over the loudspeaker, he grumbled out loud, making some critical remark, but the other passengers, who heard him, failed to react. Despite the fact that he himself was an inventor and discoverer, he was not in the least impressed by the invention of the airplane. He had irritable bowels, and he swallowed a pill.

In the heights over the Atlantic there was a storm, and the captain said, "This is your captain. Passengers are requested to fasten their seatbelts and remain in their places." As soon as the storm calmed down, the food arrived. Gruber lifted the aluminum lid from his meal and saw what it was he was supposed to eat. He was surrounded on all sides.

He hardly ate a thing, and signaled for his tray to be removed. The flight attendant who arrived was very ugly and she looked sadly at his tray and at him, as if she herself had prepared the meal. She and her colleagues had done their best to improve the conditions of the flight for the grumpy passenger in 48H, they had helped the two Americans to control the youths from Chicago, gone back and forth to bring Gruber another blanket that didn't scratch, an extra pillow, more water, more coffee.

Around him, sleep had fallen on everyone. He was amused by the fact that the flight attendant took an interest in his future wishes too: "Would you prefer beer or water to drink?" He could hardly pour the beer, because the storm wasn't really over, and there was no room for him to raise his elbows either. The beer made his stomach feel even worse, and he really needed to go to the toilet.

He tried to stand up, packed in between two sleeping sons of ex-Israelis from Chicago, and in the end he was obliged to climb over one of them, and then to take five or six steps to the tail of the plane and join the line. Although he took care to count the people in front of him, he wasn't sure that he had kept his place. As soon as he entered the little cubicle and shut himself in, the plane shook and the light instructing passengers to return to their seats and fasten their seatbelts went on again. There was an extension of the fasten seatbelt light in the toilets. Gruber actually felt rather relieved at not having to fasten any seatbelt, and he reassured himself by imagining that he wasn't in a plane in the sky but in a train in Israel traveling to Beersheba, which explained the swaying left and right.

Now he looked around at the most popular place on the flight. Everything was wet from the urinating of his all predecessors, down to the first generation. He vomited his modest meal, flushed the toilet (which made a noise, as the warning notice in Hebrew and English warned), washed his face, and again felt the stab in his irritable bowels, which symbolized anxiety with regard to the future, and outrage at what had already happened and could not be changed.

The source of the genius's agony was the sudden, simultaneous death of four thousand golden orb weavers (*Nephila maculata*), known for their strong, flexible golden webs, from which he had hoped to produce the T-suits and turn Israel into a Security Textile Power.

In the tropical regions where *Nephila maculata* originates, the inhabitants succeeded in exploiting their strong webs to make fishing nets and lines, and in South America there were attempts to use the webs of this talented spider in the manufacture of safety nets for circus acrobats.

Gruber went further.

He emerged from the toilet pale and swaying. His exhaustion was evident to all, and he himself felt that he could no longer stand being himself. A genius, sensitive, vulnerable, the joke of the week, a complete floor rag. The two Chicago youths did not wake up in the course of his efforts to return to his seat, and he collapsed into it with a sigh.

All the hopes of the Israeli scientist were pinned on an American colleague by the name of Bahat McPhee, an ex-Israeli he had met on the Internet, in the international forum of arthropod lovers. The relationship between Irad Gruber and Bahat McPhee was one of the strangest and most complicated ever formed between an Israeli living in Israel and an American-Israeli colleague.

In the beginning they asked each other ordinary questions, such as, when and where were you born, why did you leave Israel, what's new in Israel and in America, what school did you go to, what did you do in the army, how did you come to dedicate yourself to the study of the arthropods, etc.

In one of their conversations, Irad let slip to Bahat, without paying attention and without thinking, his birth date: the twenty-fifth of December. From that moment on Bahat changed her attitude toward him and became full of reverence and respect, exceeding anything he could remember even in the days when he was awarded the Israel Prize.

The meaning of the glory with which she showered him after discovering his birth date, he learned directly from her. She worshipped Rod Serling, she wanted to set up an Internet site in his memory, at the moment she didn't have the time, but soon she intended to go into low gear and do it.

"Who's Rod Serling?" asked Gruber hesitantly.

"The genius who wrote *The Twilight Zone*. You remember the series? Didn't you watch television when we were children?"

"Aah, I saw it," he said.

"You and he were born on the same day, albeit not the same year. He died in seventy something, and you're still alive."

"I'm still alive," Gruber confirmed.

After Bahat McPhee discovered that Irad Gruber and Rod Serling were born on the same day (you can never know what biographical detail will connect a man to his fellow), she not only treated him with great affection, she went much further and disclosed *secrets* to him. She too was working on increasing the productivity of the spinning glands of the golden orb weavers, and her goal was his goal: to manufacture a lightweight protective suit, flexible and effective, in an era of uncertain personal security.

The prestigious Cornell University, situated in the town of Ithaca, together with the municipality of that same town, in conjunction with other bodies she preferred not to talk about on the Internet, were funding her research. She asked who was funding his research, and he didn't mind telling her.

DURING THE PAST terrible week when all his spiders died at once while he was investigating the genome of their silk proteins, he had not spoken to her, because he was afraid she would make fun of him. Everyone knew that the spider was not a social animal, and collecting four thousand of them in a single space, however big, was asking for trouble. He knew this, but for some reason he hoped it would work out, that the spiders would not let him, Dr. Irad Gruber, down. After their death he also asked that the possibility of the spiders having been deliberately gassed be investigated, but he didn't know if anyone had bothered to check it out.

In the nights following the death of the four thousand *Nephila* he suffered from insomnia (exactly like Rod Serling), and on the third night he called her up on the ordinary telephone and told her about the catastrophe. To his astonishment she did not laugh or mock, but listened with empathy, and when he concluded his confession, she went so far as to volunteer to help him and fill him in on all her research findings to date. "You are not alone," she said to him, and his heart filled with hope. She added, "Get on a plane and come here. You won't be sorry. It's a beautiful place too."

Gruber didn't think twice. He would have traveled to any godforsaken hole in the world to save his project from capsizing. He applied to the defense minister to approve a trip to New York State, in order to meet an ex-Israeli American who for mysterious reasons was willing to donate her research findings on the golden orb weaver free, gratis, and for nothing. The defense minister was a forgiving man and he approved the trip, which seemed to him an act of despair and an escape from reality.

Gruber knew that the ministry had already approached his rivals from the Hebrew University in Jerusalem, who were working with biophysicists from Munich on producing extremely strong spider webs without spiders. From an article published in *Current Biology* he learned that the Jerusalemites had succeeded in transferring the web-producing genes, albeit not in commercial amounts, to the fruit fly *Drosophila melanogaster*. The flies had begun to produce spider webs from their saliva glands, which are equipped with giant chromosomes.

Clearly, therefore, the Jerusalemites too were intent on the mass production of spider webs, and in light of the new circumstances, they were likely to get there before him.

McPhee claimed to have made far more significant progress, but she was not willing to go into detail on the Internet or on the phone, but only face to face. He hoped all this wasn't some daydream, even though he was afraid she might be somewhat eccentric, because of her attitude toward Rod Serling, and especially because she was so proud of the fact that for a number of years he had taught communications at one of the excellent colleges in her town, Ithaca. There was something boastful too in her claim that everyone knew that Ithaca provided the best educational services in the world, about which she bragged as if she was one of the founding fathers.

But he knew that if after he met her and it all turned out to be wishful thinking, he would die in America of a stroke or cardiac arrest. He was already suffering from health problems as a result of the hell of the previous week. An irregular heart beat, an antsy feeling at the tips of his fingers, and shame, great shame. He couldn't look his biophysicists in the eye. They had spent months prying into the spinning glands of the right spiders, but apparently that wasn't enough.

Success in the mass production of spider webs was a one-way ticket to eternity, and Gruber longed to leave his mark on eternity, like Copernicus, Galileo, the inventor of the pendulum clock whose name he had forgotten, and the same with the steam engine and the small pox vaccination, Darwin, Michelangelo, and Nobel himself, who invented dynamite.

Gruber knew very well that a Nobel Prize for the invention of the ultimate protective suit was already waiting in Stockholm for the person who came to pluck it. In his mind's eye he could already see the trivia question: What is the name of the man who removed the sting from war and international terror by inventing the protective suit against deadly weapons?

But at this point reality suddenly intruded again, and the up-to-date facts overcame his being like a natural disaster, and at precisely ten thousand miles above the Atlantic, at a temperature of minus fifty degrees Celsius outside, Gruber fell into a deep depression. He tried to go to sleep but failed. Destructive thoughts ravaged and riddled his brain. His head became hollow.

If he returned from his trip to the United States empty handed . . . It would be Titanic three—if Titanic one was the disaster of the Titanic itself, and Titanic two was the movie with Leonardo DiCaprio.

In his mind's eye he saw himself coming back with nothing. And the force of the blow made him lose consciousness. The flight attendants and the passengers all thought that the person leaning back with his mouth open was sound asleep, and left him alone until an hour before landing. Only then did they grasp his situation and they shook him until he woke up and found himself looking at a doctor who was asking him if he suffered from epilepsy. Gruber replied in the negative, and the flight attendants pampered him in the hour left before landing.

And during that hour Gruber also pieced together the visions he had seen while his mind was wandering.

He had spent the time in question at a cocktail party with representatives of enlightened countries. They were angry with him and told him that the success of the protective suits, and their distribution worldwide, were paradoxically harmful to the welfare of mankind. The covering of humanity in the work of his hands would damage one of the pillars of war: the dead.

One of the guests volunteered to explain to him that the industry of mourning and bereavement employed many people in the global village, and also that there were countries in the world which were so multicultural, that grief and bereavement were the only things that kept the peace there and prevented civil war from breaking out.

"It's impossible to establish a new state every two streets and a square," said the man. And the prophet Isaiah too suddenly appeared to him toward the end of the flight, not in the shape of flesh and blood, but as an inner command, since Gruber knew that in the book of Isaiah, chapter 59, verse 6, it said, "Their webs shall not become garments, neither shall they cover themselves with their works."

The plane landed. Gruber was as wet as after aerobic activity. He stood up to take the heavy bag containing his laptop computer down from the luggage compartment.

4

THE ANESTHETIST GAVE MANDY AN ADDITIONAL SHOT IN the vein. Her upper back had already been opened up: two nice, neat cuts to the right and the left, parallel to the spinal cord.

"Unbelievable the things people do today," said the OR nurse, "a friend of a friend of mine in Ohio had a collarbone implant on both sides to improve her decolletage, and that's even before what she did to her breasts. It's insane what people do to themselves. I even heard about someone who had the backs of her hands lifted. The only operation I'd be prepared to have would be a *look* implant, but nobody's invented one yet. If they had—I'd like to have it." And after a second she added longingly, "Aaah, if only there was such thing, a look implant!"

"A look implant?" said Yagoda and a flash of mockery appeared in his sad eyes peeping over the green mask, "What for? To see a better world?"

"No, Professor. So that the look won't expose the age. All the plastic surgery on the face, and in my opinion on the body too, are useless as long as nobody's invented a look implant. The look betrays the age. People don't realize this. You can see everything in a person's look."

"Interesting, interesting," Yagoda tried to make nice, "and will it be possible to choose a different look for every day?"

"For every hour," giggled the nurse.

"That will come too, wait and see," he said, just to put an end to the conversation.

Yagoda was a Harvard graduate, and among other things he had learned there how to maintain pleasant relations with the operating team, and how to hum the consonant *M* in order to give rise to the illusion of interest and attention. On the other hand, he had also learned how to defend himself from total immersion in idle chatter, which was liable to distract him from the ongoing operation. From time to time he had to throw out an indisputable statement of fact, after which there was nothing to say. This defined him as the boss of the given operation, and set him above the rest of those present.

This time he said: "The average person is capable of saying two hundred words a minute, and the average person is capable of listening to one hundred and sixty words a minute. Which means that there will always be those who talk to the air, owing to the limitations of the average person's ability to listen. There will always be words that are wasted on thin air."

Silence fell. He didn't want to seem superior, even though if he hadn't been superior to a lot of people, he would not have become a plastic surgeon with an international reputation, as well as the assistant director of the plastic surgery department of the biggest hospital in Dresden.

WHEN HE WAS STARTING out over there, and curious and nosy people asked him what had brought him to Germany, he had replied: "Love." And this reply shut them up. There never was and never would be a more crushing reply, Yagoda knew, when addressing the question of his emigration to Germany.

Monica, whom he had met in Harvard, loved him, and for as long as the love lasted the couple had lived in the city of Hamburg, which he actually detested. He persuaded Monica to move to Cologne, and she agreed, also in the name of love. The young Yagoda felt that he had the moral right to ask her to move from town to town in *that* country, after he himself had completely given up on Israel, for her sake.

Today Yagoda thought that moving to Cologne had been a mistake. They should have moved to Munich. Cologne had shortened the life of their love, owing to circumstances and coincidences that would never have happened if they had stayed in Hamburg, or moved to Munich.

When the love between him and Monica was over, other loves came, all in this complicated country, loves which also produced children. Yagoda had four children, dispersed in different cities in Germany, corresponding to his loves.

He arrived in Dresden divorced for the third time, shortly after the fall of the wall. They offered him a job in a local hospital, and he made very good progress, even though he had no love there. In fact he was already worn out by relationships and the efforts demanded of him in order to go forward and not get bored in the relationship. He put his heart and soul into fresh approaches and holidays, but there was always friction.

Yagoda preferred Dresden to all the other cities in Germany.

In the Second World War the allied forces had bombed this city very thoroughly, and most of it was new, in relation to other big cities.

The absence of history was convenient for him.

And nevertheless he reminded himself from time to time that he was a Jew, and repeated to himself that if he had been alive then, he would have stopped being alive a long time ago.

Since coming to the city of Dresden, the doctor flourished and even if he had no love there, he didn't see it as a tragedy. Here and there he had a fling with a married nurse, and he was satisfied with this.

HE FINISHED MAKING ROOM for the new shoulder blades. According to the concept of the state-of-the-art operation, there was no need to remove the old shoulder blades, since they were so worn out anyway, and they could even serve as a bed for the new ones.

The new ones would hide the old ones as long as she lived.

The two prosthetic shoulder blades were brought on a tray, boiling with sterilization. They were made of tough plastic material, in a shade of very pale light green. Their size and sharpness had been decided by Mandy weeks before the operation, according to examples he had sent her on the Internet.

Dr. Yagoda was about to put them in place, join them to the muscles, and the muscles to the bones and tendons, as required—and then to close up Mrs. Gruber, one of many who could not, on any account, face the effects of the passing of time.

IT WAS NOT LONG since Mandy had buried her mother Audrey, who was eighty-two when she died. With her own eyes she had observed the process of her decline, and if she so wished, she could also have documented it in a special notebook. She had noticed how Audrey grew shorter and shorter, and how the little hump on her back made it increasingly bent, although it never reached the terrible angle of ninety degrees. She saw the hair on her head dwindling to a tuft that no hairdresser in the world could set into a hairdo that lasted more than ten minutes.

Even though she saw her mother almost every day, and everybody knows that if you see someone so frequently, you don't notice changes, Mandy noted to herself that her mother's face was shrinking further and further toward some unknown point. Her neck too, once the most magnificent neck in Rhodesia, and then in the Levant, was shrinking fast, while at the same time the handsome contours of the south of her face melted into the skin of a wobbly double chin.

All this was accompanied by the retreat of the mind of a woman who until the age of sixty-something could multiply seven hundred and forty-eight by nine-point-nine in a matter of seconds in her head. She herself reported on a fog that was gradually covering her lucidity, and said that she had to rely on "ever-diminishing areas" in order to communicate her thoughts.

In the last two years of her life, Audrey Greenholtz agreed to leave the apartment at 18 Arlozorov Street and move into a renovated old-age home on Einstein Street. But once she was there she never stopped complaining about how miserable she was, and how she suffered from the mere presence of the other old people, who made her feel depressed and hopeless.

She claimed that their appearance alone was enough to age her and even to kill her, and rebuked her daughter for removing her from her home.

Mandy reminded her that she had offered to get her "someone" to help her day and night, and that she was the one who refused and preferred the retirement home. But Audrey ignored her.

"There are some people who, even when they grow old, nobody throws them out of their homes," she said to her daughter and made her feel guilty. And she also said that she had wandered the world enough, and the proof of how far she had traveled was that she came from a country that only existed on old maps.

After a short time, as if to close ranks with the other Einstein residents, she deteriorated greatly, until in the last year of her life it happened—not often, but it happened—that she forgot the nature of her relationship to her daughter. Were they sisters? Was she her neighbor from 18 Arlozorov, who had come to visit her yesterday, the one whose husband was a compulsive key-holder collector?

Audrey's imagination housed marginal characters from the past, who were suddenly illuminated from a new angle, such as, for example, the Singer technician with whom she had been in love at the end of the seventies, something which so far as Mandy knew had never actually happened. Sometimes she would ask Mandy when she had returned from Detroit, because a textile conference had once taken place there years ago and Mandy had attended it on behalf of the factory to pick up ideas for fabrics which they would then commission from the textile factory they worked with without fear of impurities or fear of anything else.

When Mandy was supposed to fly home, a big strike broke out and her return was delayed, and Audrey was very worried about her. Lirit was then twelve years old, Gruber was wrapped up in himself, and the grandmother was afraid that Mandy would never return and the burden of caring for the two children would fall to her.

This wasn't completely irrational, because for a few days there was no telephone connection with Mandy, and it was only with the help of the Israeli consulate in Detroit that they succeeded in locating her.

It was a very big strike, although there have been bigger ones since. In any case, when it came to an end, the economy was no longer the same as it was before.

ON THE LAST NIGHT of her life, after she had sentenced Mandy to not being the third generation of female loneliness, and even threatened her that she would haunt her from heaven if she introduced radical changes in Nighty-Night, she murmured the names of outstanding members of the ultra-Orthodox clientele of the pajama factory in the sixties and seventies.

After she died, Mandy sank into a permanent state of depression. It seemed that she did everything with an apathetic shrug of her shoulders, without a real smile. Suddenly she understood that nature was cruel and it didn't give anybody a discount, not even her. To her increasing annoyance and resentment she discovered that the contours of the bottom of her face, too, were disappearing into a new chin, which had suddenly appeared out of nowhere, with no justification, after all her efforts not to put on weight. And she also discovered that a layer of fat of more than a centimeter thick had grown on her back, making her beautiful spine hollow and disappointing. Her vision too was deteriorating. When she looked at the notices she had published in the papers announcing her mother's death, the small letters and even some of the big ones were blurred.

At the optician's office next to her house, they told her that she was plus two in her right eye and plus one and three-quarters in her left eye, and she needed bifocals for driving and reading.

In order to compensate herself, Mandy bought gorgeous glasses for $675.

ABOUT A YEAR after her mother's death Mandy went back to cherishing the vain hope that while the march toward extinction was self-evident, and it was clear that she would grow old and die like everybody else, perhaps *she* would be given special consideration "over there," wherever that might be, and the process would be softened in her case. "Over there" they must know how important external appearances, aesthetics, were to her, and therefore they would meet her halfway. Perhaps because of her CV: after all, she had been second to the queen of the class in primary school, and quite popular in high school too.

At the same time she began to change her diet to a strict regime: no milk, meat, fish, eggs, bread, or coffee—only fruit, vegetables, and some seaweed or other. In the morning she drank wheat grass that she pulverized and made into juice herself, and during the day she made sure to swallow all the most up-to-date vitamins and omegas on the market.

Before she embarked on the series of plastic surgeries, she gave the cosmetics companies a chance, and spent a fortune on their promising products, especially one which was made of caviar (Creme Caviar), which she ordered on the Internet from a store in Los Angeles and paid $1,570 for.

In those days the home page on her computer, at home and at work, was the website of a famous and innovative cosmetics company, and she even downloaded screen savers from their site with all kinds of variations on the company's logo.

Dael's conscription sent her back to her ordinary news site home page and to a simple Nivea face cream, having put the rest in the hands of her chosen plastic surgeons. She chose them with great care after investigation, and she also made inquiries as to anesthetics, but since she was unable to get her hands on any, she made do with various tranquilizers, which she took care to vary after a few months because she thought that this way she would save herself from getting addicted.

To date Mandy had spent $68,000 on plastic surgery, and it was clear to her that as long as Dael was in the army and he still had time to be served—this was what her life would look like. About her death, she refrained from thinking.

IN THE MEDICAL FRONTLINE OR there was unexpected stress. The saturation level of the oxygen in Mandy's blood began to drop. Seventy-five. There were a few minutes of very professional and controlled alarm, and in the end the operating team succeeded in stabilizing the patient and the operation continued.

But so far as Dr. Yagoda was concerned, those stressful moments during the course of the surgery on Mrs. Amanda Gruber concluded a chapter in his life. He would no longer perform plastic surgeries in Israel. He would no longer come to Israel at all, not even for the Passover Seder or Rosh Hashanah with his sister in Nahariya. His connection with the State of Israel was at an end.

Yagoda was so alarmed because for the first time since he had been living on his own without any love, he had nearly lost a patient on the operating table. He connected the drama in the OR to the country in which it had taken place, and to the grievous cardiac condition of its inhabitants, and decided to return to Germany the next morning. He considered giving up surgery altogether, and restricting himself to pre-operative consultations in a private clinic.

Before leaving he glanced at Mandy's chart. There was nothing in it about sensitivity to any anesthetic whatsoever. He left the OR, ripped off his mask and gloves, threw them all into the nearest bin, stopped at the first telephone he came across, dialed information, and asked for the number of Lufthansa in Israel. At Lufthansa they answered in German, told him that a flight for Frankfurt was departing in five hours' time, and promised him that he would make it. There were two places left in business class.

Dr. Yagoda felt that he was advancing with resolute steps toward a turning point in his life. From Frankfurt he would take a train home, announce that he was taking a month's leave, and disappear for two months at least. Who knows, perhaps in those two months he would find a new love, which would shoot jets of hope into his empty soul, and he would be filled with new strength. The German doctor had learned to exploit his love affairs to store up energy for times when the daily grind turns you into a carob pod that's been lying in the desert for a year.

EIGHT HOURS AFTER the complicated operation, which had succeeded in the end, but had cost the surgeon his peace of mind, Mandy lay on her stomach in the nice room they had given her, bandaged and immobilized in a number of places, but open eyed and completely *au fait.*

They had promised her five stars, and she had nothing to complain about because all she could see of the five stars was a bit of white carpet, but she couldn't tell if it was wall-to-wall, because she couldn't see the end. If she had turned her head to the right, the patient would have been able to see more of the carpet and part of a cupboard. But turning her head involved excruciating pain, and she had to call the nurse to hold her hand when she turned it.

Since eating in her position was impossible, she received nourishment and liquids and all kind of medications through a variety of tubes. In intimate matters they tried to make things as easy as possible for her. But there were limitations and grave embarrassments. Mandy thought that this time she had gone too far.

LIRIT CAME TO VISIT her, after going home to change her clothes. In the end she had paid a flying visit to the factory after the Jacuzzi. She and her mother had agreed that she would come every day to report on what had happened in the factory. She arrived at the hospital dressed atrociously, as usual. Her daughter was revealed to Mandy's eyes in flat yellow shoes, flimsy as ballet shoes, a short billowing white skirt, and a very tightly fitting rayon tank top, pale yellow with white flowers, with straps that tied behind the neck and an extra piece of material in the area of the stomach that was also supposed to billow in the breeze.

Her shoulder blades were exquisite, as usual. But what suddenly infuriated Amanda, after she asked her to bend down so that she could see all of her, were the two braids which were thrown back, but one of them kept falling forward and Lirit would flip it back again. The two braids were thick, long, and brown, like Pocahontas.

"Are you doing this to me on purpose? Braids?" hissed Mandy from the depths of her strange position.

"Mother, stop it. You're lying there like this, and that's what you have to say to me? I already prepared an answer in case you had something to say about *my* shoulder blades. When will you realize that I'm twenty-two years old, and that I have the right to wear braids?"

"You look like a whore from the *Little House on the Prairie*. And it annoys me that precisely when I'm lying in the hospital dying of pain, you turn up like this to tease me. It shows a lack of consideration."

"Ex-cuse me," said Lirit and she undid her braids.

"Are you trying to tell me that you went to work like that? We work with a religious clientele!"

"Mother, anyone would think that you hadn't just had surgery. Usually you're much quieter after surgery, and it's fun to come and visit you. Maybe it's the only quality time we have together. Do you want to ruin this too?"

Mandy was silent for a moment, and it seemed she had calmed down.

"A short page is what suits you best, like I used to have your hair cut when you were a little girl. You have an amazing neck and a perfect collarbone—a short page is what would show them off best. Take advantage of what you have as long as you have it."

"I don't want a page," said Lirit for the umpteenth time since the age of five.

"So don't have one. At least we've agreed on the braids."

LIRIT WENT ON unbraiding her hair, and suddenly she became worried because Shlomi hadn't called her all day. How come? Her mother's having such complicated surgery—never mind that she wasn't there either—and he doesn't call to ask how she is. What is this? It's the behavior of a psychopath, that's what! Is Shlomi a psychopath? she asked herself and she didn't know the answer.

Mandy saw her daughter sending a text message on her cell phone.

"Just a minute," said Lirit as she wrote. "I'm just sending this and then I'll finish undoing the braids."

She sent the message and finished undoing her braids.

"Okay now?" she asked a moment later, and bent down so Mandy could see.

"Yes."

Lirit asked her mother if she was in pain now. Amanda said that she was in pain all the time, it was just a question of how much. Lirit said it was logical for her to be in pain, after all she had undergone surgery today, and she looked at the dripping infusion. The sight had a slightly hypnotic effect on her, and she sank into herself.

"They're giving me antibiotics," said Mandy. "I had a fever an hour ago. You know that the doctor has already gone back to Germany? I don't know why he's in such a hurry."

"Another operation, what do you think," said Lirit. "The

only thing that interests them is money. You're acting not quite normally."

"Yes, I feel a little strange too. Vo-mi-ting dish!" yelled Mandy.

"Mommy!" cried Lirit and she leaped for the kidney-shaped green dish.

"Here, here it is . . ." Lirit brought the dish to Mandy's mouth.

Mandy succeeded in raising herself a little while mumbling in ex-Rhodesian English, and vomited all the liquids. Then she closed her eyes.

"They gave me too much anesthetic. Disgusting."

The patient fell back onto her stomach with the help of her daughter, moaning all the time:

"Ai, ai, ai . . ."

Without opening her eyes and with great difficulty she said to herself:

"I want to wear bare-backed dresses again . . . but it hurts so much. Never mind . . . it will pass . . . it's not a disease, it's only plastic surgery."

And to Lirit she said, "You understand, darling Lirit, I couldn't bear having my shoulder blades rubbed out and a back as flat as a plate with a canal for a spine. I said to myself, forget the spine, but the shoulder blades! I couldn't take it. And now look what a position I'm stuck in . . ."

Tears poured from her eyes and were absorbed straight into the white sheet, on which was written in decorative Hebrew letters: Medical Frontline.

"In two days' time I'll be allowed to get up, to lie on my back. Everything will be all right," she consoled herself.

"Come here a minute, Liritkeleh, help me, dear. I want to turn my head to the other side. It's hard, it hurts, but I'm sick of having it on the same side all the time. All I need are bedsores on my face!"

As gently as she could, but with a little sting of malice, her daughter said:

"Mother, you have to flow with time. To accept the change."

"When you grow up, *you* accept the change," muttered Mandy.

"But you have to. It's stupid to fight the wheels of time . . ."

"How's Dael?" cried Mandy suddenly and stretched a tiny bit, because of the pain. It was only now that she remembered this worry. "Was there any exchange of fire mentioned on the news? Did they say an Israeli was killed in the shooting, his family not yet notified?"

"Everything's fine, I spoke to him fifteen minutes ago."

"Thank God," said Mandy. "That's what I feared the most. I'm under the anesthetic, and something happens to him."

Lirit thought: What difference does it make if she's anesthetized when something happens to him? What's she missing that's so urgent for her to know?

"What about your father?" Mandy sighed again.

"He's probably still up in the sky," said Lirit and looked at her mother lying on her stomach as helpless as an overturned tortoise. There was a lot of compassion in the daughter's look. And on the other hand, to be on the safe side, she thanked God that she was still young with her whole life before her, and not like her mother who was buried in a pajama factory. She, whatever her situation in life might be, still had a lot of opportunities!

5

BAHAT MCPHEE WAS AN ABSENTMINDED WOMAN, WHICH led to deficiencies in her orientation in space. In her late forties the condition worsened, to such an extent that she would lose her car even when she parked it outside the underground parking lots she hated. Not long ago she had lost it when she parked (by mistake) two streets away from her home, since the parking space reserved for her was occupied, and it never occurred to her to appeal to the authorities.

One day, in the middle of searching for her car in minus four of the underground parking lot, McPhee had a revelation. She understood that people's terror of death was a post-traumatic phenomenon. Death was so terrible that their minds consented to remembering only the fear they experienced when it happened, and not the event itself.

McPhee knew that difficult and central events in a person's life were erased from the center of the memory and stationed like soldiers on the periphery, in the margins of the margins, to keep them from returning and upsetting people again. She too had black holes in her memory, and perhaps they were responsible for the damage to her orientation in space.

During the same revelation on minus four, row seventeen, the professor of zoology also understood that we were not given souls in order to wax lyrical on the fear of their extinction and the difficulties of life. She knew nature, this wasn't how it behaved. In nature nothing got lost. Including the soul. She noticed that while she found it difficult to believe in the existence of God, she could really connect to the Divine Presence.

Armed with these insights Bahat McPhee began to study at Hebrew Union College, at first on the Internet, and later also on short trips to New York.

She was a very lonely, bitter woman, and it was to be expected that the Divine Presence would send her revelations from time to time. Most of the hours of the day she spent in her lab, riveted to the golden silk webs and their manufacturers, the *Nephila maculata*.

Recently, with the lack of significant progress in her research, the prestigious Cornell University had brought in a Hispanic biophysicist residing in Ithaca, fifteen years younger than she was, named Mario Salazar. During the first two weeks a passionate love affair broke out between the two, but it quickly petered out. To the credit of the participants in the lightning romance, let it be said that they did not suffer from mutual rejection after the storm subsided, but became practical, concentrated, brisk, and the research which had previously faltered suddenly charged full steam ahead, with results she was happy to pass on to the Israeli inventor.

MCPHEE WAS BORN in Israel, in the green suburb of Ramat Aviv, in the small Shimoni Street, leading off the big Reading Street. She lived in with her parents, Reudor and Madeleine Segal, and her arachnophobic sister, Shoham, in a two-and-a-half-roomed ground-floor apartment.

At the end of the sixties, when she was twelve, the family went to San Francisco as emissaries on behalf of the state. Reudor Segal was a senior civil servant.

In San Francisco the Segals settled down for two years in a lovely apartment on a hill, not far from Chinatown. From the windows the two sisters, sweet Bahat and Shoham, looked out at the Golden Gate Bridge and tried to guess the meaning of the elusive landscape on the other side of the river.

During this period their parents were caught up in the beatnik revolution, and in the framework of their search for the right way of life, they became acquainted with Shivananda Yoga, after which they were never the same.

At the end of his mission the state fired Reudor, due to budget cuts, and he sank into unemployment and depression. He even started to talk about divorce. Madeleine, who was at her wit's end in trying to prevent the melancholy Reudor from leaving her with two children and a bit of lawn adjoining the front porch, suggested that okay, he could start proceedings that would end in divorce, but in the meantime they should practice yoga on the aforementioned strip of lawn. The yoga brought them together, and they improved from day to day. After a few months they even started to give lessons privately, on the lawn and inside the house, and afterward they got permission to work in the Shimoni Street air-raid shelter, because luckily for them there wasn't a war at the time. They taught five days a week and stopped talking about getting divorced. About a year after Reudor lost his job, their financial situation stabilized and they opened the first yoga school of its kind, which they called Splendor on the Lawn. The school had dozens of students. Some of them preferred her, and others preferred him, but there was no jealousy between them, only harmony, and it seemed that they had reached safe harbors, at least for the time being.

Every day at dawn they did an hour of yoga on the lawn. Lightly and flexibly, they executed all kinds of positions (asanas) which released energetic blocks, including head stands without a wall. For a long time the two of them were capable of remaining upside down between heaven and earth, thereby enabling the blood to reach every capillary in their brains, steeping themselves in a pleasant relaxation. In the morning hours they would cook vegetarian food for the children who attended the Alliance Israelite school, and around noon they would go to open the doors of Splendor on the Lawn.

Their daughters Bahat and Shoham were obliged to become parasites insofar as they always went to visit their friends, but never invited their friends home because they were afraid that their mother or their father would suddenly stand on their heads, and they would become pariahs.

The yoga kept the family together, but isolated the two girls.

Financial security made it possible for the parents to develop the art of conversation between themselves, and to pass on to their students what they discovered or invented. And indeed they invented various expressions to convey to their students what they should do and feel.

For example, the Segals were the first in the country to say, "I'm speaking from a place of . . ." They were the ones who invented the culture of "place" in the Hebrew language, and it was from there that they spoke to their students during the lesson and after it. All kinds of abstractions turned into places. There was a place of pain, a place of loneliness and frustration, a place of wanting to help, a place of compassion, and so on. They were the first to recognize that someone speaking from a place of anger was unable to talk to someone speaking from a place of acceptance. The widespread use of this term indirectly helped hundreds of psychologists throughout the country to communicate with their clients, and vice versa. Neither the state nor the Language Academy saw fit to reward the Segals for their efforts, but they were serene and it didn't bother them.

Their dream, which came from a place of daydreams, was of course to go to India for as many years as possible, and there to learn how to live to the ripe old age of ninety-something.

ON THE DAY that Shoham received an exemption from guard and kitchen duty due to her terror of spiders—arachnophobia—Madeleine and Reudor set out for Mysore in India to learn and internalize another brand of yoga (Ashtanga).

Bahat was already planning her post-army trip.

At first things in India were almost perfect, but after a few weeks the Segals met a local yogi called Helen. Three months after they landed in India, Reudor ran away to Rishikesh with his new love Helen, who was also a guru.

Helen was more supple than Madeleine and more advanced than her in yoga, even though she was eight years older than Madeleine. She had been born in India, and had practiced from the age of three. Her parents had arrived there as colonialists in the framework of the expansion of the British Empire, and they had all returned to England in the framework of its contraction, after India received its independence. Helen had returned with them, but after a decade she wearied of the West and went back to India for good.

Her loneliness, her wisdom, her smile, and her agility captivated Reudor, who in any case was beginning to be bored to death with his wife.

After the separation from Reudor, Madeleine suffered a terrible crisis, which she overcame under the devoted care of nuns in Mysore. When she recovered her prana, she returned to Israel and to her daughters with the intention of cherishing them and remedying the injustices of the past. But Bahat had already set out on her coast-to-coast trip to America with her high school friend, Hagit, and Shoham had studied to be a midwife, and gone to work in the Yoseftal Hospital in Eilat.

This being the case, Madeleine Segal took up residence on her own in the ground floor apartment in green Ramat Aviv, and she made no attempt to renew the glory days of the yoga school, with the result that she soon fell into severe economic distress—something she had never experienced before.

And then the third blow fell. Bahat, who had set out for no more than a three month coast-to-coast trip, did not return to Israel, having fallen in love with a local boy from some university town in the far north of New York State. One daughter in Eilat, one daughter in northern New York, a husband in India—thus Madeleine summed up her achievements in life.

She spent hours on the phone to Bahat, imploring her to leave her local lover and return to her motherland and her mother, to what was left of her mother, she really needed her, and what did she have to do in upstate New York anyway. But Bahat was determined to be independent and even more original than her parents.

When Bahat's traveling companion Hagit returned to Israel, she went to visit Madeleine and told her how Bahat's desertion had come about. Madeleine recognized pure evil in her, but she sat quietly and listened to the wicked girl.

The two girls had been on their way to New York, to spend their last week there. Hagit just wanted to pass through Ithaca, because she was a bookworm addicted to useless knowledge. She had read in the thick guide book that they had bought at the beginning of their trip, which was already tattered with use, that little Ithaca was full of secondhand bookshops, and she wanted to pick up a few classics. Her English was excellent, much better than Bahat's, even though she had never lived in an English speaking country.

For some reason Hagit was interested in the history of the United States, and at this point in the conversation she explained to Madeleine that in the past Ithaca had been called the city of sin, and even Sodom, because in its early days at the beginning of the nineteenth century, all kinds of lowlifes had lived there. Only after the Civil War between the North and South did the licentious town become a place of refinement, education, and beauty, with a highly developed community life, churches, and a great awareness of the importance of education in the life of the individual and the town. Ithaca's educational institutions, especially Cornell University, were well-known today all over the world.

As far as Hagit knew, Bahat's lover, Randall McPhee, a good-looking guy with long, curly hair, was going to study at Cornell University, science or Italian, after graduating from college with distinction.

"What does the place look like?" asked Madeleine.

"It's a beautiful place. Lots of atmosphere. There's a big lake with a stormy river running out of it. Huge waterfalls.

Lots of green. It's very cold in winter. Randall promised your daughter she wouldn't be cold. But there's something strange about the place. It's hard to explain. Have you ever heard of Rod Serling?"

"No."

"Do you watch *The Twilight Zone* on television?"

"Sure," said Madeleine, who saw everything there was to see on television.

"It's he who wrote the script for the series, and he based it on the atmosphere there."

"What do you say!"

"Do you know Nabokov?"

"The writer?"

"He taught at Cornell."

"And what did you say was Bahat's boyfriend's name?"

"Randall. It's a Southern name. The family is originally from Texas. You don't know how hard I tried to persuade her to come back to Israel and not to stay in that place, and with a Texan too. Look, Mrs. Segal, your daughter slept with a lot of men in America, and when she met Randall I thought it was just another fling. I didn't know it was eternal love."

"Eternal love?" asked Madeleine.

"That's what your daughter said."

"Do you think they'll get married?"

"I'm sure they will," said Hagit.

"Do you think I should go there and try to persuade her to come home?"

"I can't really see the point, Mrs. Segal. I tried everything. Your daughter's head over heels in love with him. And you know her. There's nothing anyone can do. Maybe she'll come to her senses and come home, and maybe not. But I promise you that *I'll* come and visit you sometimes," she said when she spotted a tear in Madeleine's right eye.

"I haven't even got the money for a plane ticket. And I don't want to go there and impose myself on them. Reudor took everything, everything." Now the tears were streaming down her face.

Hagit stayed in the little apartment on Shimoni Street for another half-hour and ate dried fruits past their sell-by date. She didn't have anything encouraging to say to Madeleine, and so she promised her again that she would come and visit her once a month. This promise brought no consolation, especially since her daughter's traveling companion forgot about her promise and failed to keep her word.

MADELEINE SANK into profound melancholy with fits of apathy, and spent the rest of her life watching television, which improved a lot over the years. The number of channels rose from one to two, and then to many, and together with this expansion the interchannel competition increased as well. Madeleine put on a lot of weight, and needless to say, she no longer did any twists or stretches, and standing on her head was obviously out of the question, even against a wall. Her head could no longer bear the weight. Things worked out well for Shoham in Eilat, she completed a course in deep-sea diving, talked all the time about corals and coral reefs, and said that when she had a daughter she would call her Coral. On the rare occasions when she came to visit her mother, she noticed that the thin, supple woman had turned into an overweight couch potato. She tried to talk her into moving to Eilat to be close to her, but she knew there was no chance. She would not move from that couch until her dying day.

6

AT THE BEGINNING OF THE SIXTIES, STANLEY AND SAMAN-
tha McPhee, Randall's parents, came to Ithaca from a little
town in Texas, because they wanted to give their children a
good, Northern, enlightened education, without the oppressive complexes of *the history of the South*. They didn't want
their children to grow up with inferiority complexes, and
to have to change their southern accent whenever they met
anyone from the North and encounter forgiving, patronizing
looks.

After years of practice in the prestigious town, Stanley
and Samantha succeeded in almost completely effacing their
accent, and planned that the next generation, headed by Randall, would bury it forever.

Stanley and Samantha wanted to invest in the northern
branch of the McPhee family, and so they wanted five children, including Randall. But the only child born to them was
Randall, because six or seven times Samantha miscarried in
the third month of her pregnancy.

The doctors in the Woman's Health Center in Ithaca
could not explain why such a healthy woman was unable to
bring her pregnancies to term. And the doctors in New York
they consulted for a second opinion couldn't explain it either.

THE FAMILIES OF BOTH Stanley and Samantha McPhee (née Griffith) were members of AHS (American Hibiscus Society), and in Texas where they lived, the members of these families were considered fanatics on the subject. After their day jobs they devoted themselves to breeding improved new strains of the *Hibiscus rosa-sinensis*, and to inventing other exotic strains, in shades of near-black or pure white, with hearts that changed color three times over the summer.

Stanley and Samantha had met at a big exhibition of new hibiscus strains, and fallen in love.

When they moved to Ithaca, they took with them a few fine rare strains for their large garden, but most of them died in the first frost of November.

Samantha was furious with her new husband for not thinking about it in advance and not setting up a hibiscus hothouse equipped with the heaters and humidifiers required for a tropical plant originating in Hawaii.

In spite of her pregnant state, she carried the big pots containing the surviving bushes into the house, and instructed her husband to set up the above-mentioned hothouse in the big backyard and equip it with everything required.

Setting up the hothouse and operating it cost the couple a fortune, and in order to pay for it and also to earn a living, they opened a florist shop in downtown Ithaca, and next to it a secondhand bookstore. They called the florist shop Some Flowers and the bookstore Book Report. The income from the two stores minus the high costs of the hothouse provided the couple and their son Randall with a good living, but they still felt an inexplicable emptiness.

Accordingly they threw themselves heart and soul into a

purpose—Samantha into Randall, and Stanley into the search for a hibiscus unlike anything ever seen before: as blue or black as possible, with a psychedelic heart.

RANDALL MCPHEE KISSED Bahat Segal for the first time among the strange blooms produced by his father Stanley. Two days later Bahat drove her friend Hagit to the Syracuse airport to fly to New York City and from there to Israel. They didn't speak the whole way.

Randall's parents weren't crazy about their only son's choice and stayed aloof. Bahat wasn't bothered. After her alternative childhood in Shimoni street in the green suburb of Ramat Aviv, and in San Francisco, she was a girl full of self-confidence and she knew very well how to get along on her own, and she even took a historical masochistic pleasure in the stupid condescension of her Presbyterian mother-in-law.

Her father-in-law, Stanley McPhee, admired Richard Nixon with all his heart and soul, and a portrait of Nixon went on hanging in their home even after the Watergate scandal broke out. Bahat saw that her in-laws were hard-core Republicans, and nevertheless she went to study botany at Cornell University because she thought, who knows, perhaps one day *she* would succeed in creating new strains of hibiscus, to the delight of Stanley and Samantha, leading to the fall of the interracial barrier that Bahat actually did her best to encourage: she saw it fitting to begin many critical remarks about their thinking and way of life with the words, "We Jews . . ."

Bahat did well in her studies, and got into the subject of the hibiscus as if there weren't any other flowers in the world. Even though she found botany rather boring, she completed her first degree in two years. At the same time exactly, Randall completed his BA in Latin and Italian, and planned to get out of the hibiscus business to set up as a translator of these languages into English.

At the end of these two years, during which she had also worked in the family stores, Bahat switched to zoology, where she found herself far more than in botany because everything was more dynamic and dramatic.

Her master's she did on arthropods, and her doctorate on the *Nephila*, weavers of the strongest webs in the world. Her sister Shoham had recovered from her arachnophobia by the time she completed her army service and the two of them corresponded, thus Bahat learned about Shoham's success as a midwife on the coral reef in Eilat, where she had even developed a new technique.

Two daughters were born to the mixed-race couple Randall and Bahat: the first was called Sara, and the second Ruth—two names which did not clash with either religion or descent, so that the girls wouldn't have identity problems either in the United States, North or South, or in Israel, if and when they ever decided to go back, even if only on a trip to discover their roots.

Obviously the girls received the best education in the world, thanks to the excellent educational system in the town which their grandparents migrated to for precisely this reason. They were both very spoiled, too much so in Bahat's opinion, but she didn't really have a say in the matter because Samantha took over Sara and Ruth as if they were her own daughters, and Bahat knew that even if she wanted to go back to Israel with the girls, they wouldn't cooperate with her because of their grandmother.

AFTER TEN YEARS of marriage, on her thirty-first birthday, Bahat caught Randall on a table in the family hothouse next to one of big heaters, screwing Emily Boston, his first love from the age of fourteen. The two of them had not anticipated her arrival, since Pa had gone to rest and Bahat was supposed to be in the store helping Ma, or at most, sitting at home and reading an academic article about capillary physiology.

Later, Bahat discovered that Randall had returned to the bosom of Emily Boston soon after Ruth was born, in other words the affair had been going on for nearly seven years.

Randall promised Bahat that he would stop seeing Emily, but he was wasting his breath, because Bahat wanted a divorce, and Randal married Emily Boston.

After the divorce, Randall and Emily Boston moved to Boston, to a two-hundred-year-old house overlooking the river, where the plumbing kept breaking down and the repairs cost a fortune.

Randall's parents stayed in Ithaca until the day they died, which was not long ago, one after the other, and they saw it fit to leave their house to their granddaughters, but until the girls reached the age of twenty-one, their mother could do whatever she liked with it.

Ostensibly Bahat could have gone back to Israel with her daughters, who had since understood that she was their real mother and they had better listen to her, but Bahat was deep into her research on the *Nephila*, funded by the Ithaca Municipality, Cornell University, the Pentagon, and the French Ministry of Health. This being the case, the girls went to college, one to study mathematics and the other fractal geometry, and they lived in a rented apartment, while downtown Bahat became acquainted with her loneliness. She operated the stores from a distance, by means of hired workers, and to tell the truth she didn't really care about the business anymore, as long as they brought in what was expected of them every month.

In those sad days a Reform synagogue called Tikkun v'Or was opened in Ithaca, and Bahat found some consolation in it, especially in the Kabbalat Shabbat at the beginning of the Sabbath and the Havdalah at the end, even though the latter was sometimes held before the Sabbath was actually over. She liked singing the prayers without an American accent and in a loud voice, so that all the Reform Jews would hear and learn.

MCPHEE'S MAIN ACHIEVEMENT with the golden orb weavers to date was the doubling and tripling of the number of spinning glands on the abdomen on the female spinner, and she had even interfered with the control mechanism of the gene, forcing the female *Nephila* spiders to spin more and more, faster and faster.

She worked day and night to increase the spinning rate, but she devoted her weekends to attending services at Tikkun v'Or, and recently she had even spoken to one of the regular worshippers, an architect by profession who had taken part in designing the synagogue, about saying a prayer to the Divine Presence for the wellbeing of her daughters and the success of a very important experiment, without going into detail about it due to the highly confidential classification of the project.

Now the arachnologist McPhee stood in the arrivals hall of the Syracuse Airport, holding a yellow cardboard sign on which was written with a black marker in Hebrew "Irad Gruber," with a drawing of a spider underneath it, spinning its web from the last *r* in "Gruber."

She was wearing her best clothes and her hair had been dyed to the roots, because she wanted their meeting to be something big.

She was worried about the identification. Not that she was afraid of espionage or some kind of swindle, she just wanted to identify the Israeli as quickly as possible and drive him home with her so he could rest, the guy must be asleep on his feet.

He had sent her his photograph by email, but photographs can be misleading.

7

BUT WHEN THE TIME CAME, BAHAT HAD NO DOUBT AT ALL. She would have recognized him even if he had arrived on a Jumbo Jet instead of the little blue American Airlines plane. He advanced toward her, full of aches and pains, barely able to carry himself and his briefcase, dragging the medium-sized wheeled suitcase behind him. Bahat threw the placard with his name on it into the litter bin, walked straight up to him, and said in Hebrew:

"Sha*lom*, sha*lom*, welcome. Give me your case, you look exhausted. Soon everything will be all right, don't worry."

Gruber looked at her with an astonishment that embarrassed her. What had he expected? she asked herself.

They shook hands and felt a mutual aversion, stemming from the fact that they were strangers after all, but then, as if in response to a signal agreed upon in advance, they both began behaving according to accepted norms of a business meeting. Communication which was ostensibly personal, but on the most general and boring level.

"Boy, am I exhausted," replied Gruber, and noticed that she had dyed her hair, even her scalp was brown, "I feel as if I'm on my last legs."

"Everything will be all right," said Bahat, and took over the job of dragging the wheeled suitcase, too. She tried to match her pace to his, which was slower than hers. "You have nothing to worry about. You can relax after all the tension of the journey."

"My problem is my back," Gruber informed her, "I think that my entire spine is dislocated."

"We'll see what we can do about it," said Bahat and smiled at him.

Naturally they got a bit lost, because even though Bahat had written down exactly where she had parked her car, and also the color of the row where it was parked, she had lost the note with all these important details on it. And so the inevitable moments followed, during which she stood still and felt the familiar foolish feeling while she searched miserably for the lost note, even the color of which she had suddenly forgotten. While not yet not admitting to herself that she was becoming sclerotic even before reaching the age of fifty, she let out an impatient breath and shook her head in a gesture of annoyance with herself because on no account did she want to expose her sclerosis to the visiting scientist. Luckily, in the end she found the note, in the back pocket of her jeans, the pocket in which she had kept important things as a child and as a girl in the army. She thanked some historical self and changed her mood completely, from nervous embarrassment to something new and challenging, and by the time they reached her beautiful car she was in high spirits and filled him in on the doubts she was having at that very moment: whether to take him home first and then to the masseur, or first to the masseur and then home. In the end she decided on her own initiative, since at that moment in time Gruber was simply passive. He wasn't interested, he wasn't listening to her, and she decided that while he was getting a massage, she would take the briefcase and the suitcase home. It wasn't far, it was all downtown.

IN THE CLEAN and freshened up car (for she had washed it that same day and thrown out all the rubbish that had accumulated on the back seat), she told him that lately she had been forgetting things and that she was worried.

Her Hebrew sounded strange to him. Something about the accent seemed wrong. Her *r* was a little too pronounced, perhaps to hide the American *r* she had picked up. Her voice jarred on him too. He didn't listen to what she was saying, and instructed himself to remain passive and hope for the best. This was the category of mental activity demanded of him. And the decision enabled him to sink into himself.

Bahat paid at the exit from the parking lot and joined the traffic without any problems. Now she fell silent. She wasn't stupid either. Not only was she a genius from the intellectual point of view, she also possessed enough natural sensitivity to appraise the limits of the personality of the person next to her, and she sensed that somebody here demanded the maximum and maybe more, whether it existed or not.

She grasped that in his essence he prevented her own being from expanding to the dimensions she was used to: *her* maximum.

She expelled her breath in disappointed resignation to the situation, which in any case was irreversible. The guy had come all the way from Israel, and now he was here and she had to take care of him and finish what she had started, in the spirit of the saying "Anyone embarking on a mitzvah is commanded to complete it."

Sometimes Jewish expressions popped into Bahat's mind,

and lately, since she had been studying to become a Reform rabbi at the Hebrew Union College, she had even felt haunted by these quotations, such as: "Who is a hero," "A word is enough for the wise," "Think before you act." And in the end, after saying to herself "Let not him that girds on his armor boast himself as he that puts it off," she turned to the man sitting next to her and asked:

"How was the flight from New York?"

"Ghastly by any reckoning. Bumpy all the way, like being on the cable railway to the top of Masada."

"And was the flight from Israel ghastly too?"

"That was a nightmare of a different kind. Ugly flight attendants, disgusting food with your neighbor's face stuck in your tray, and toilets that haven't been cleaned since the invention of the airplane."

"I understand," said Bahat and looked glum as a sign of sympathy. "But all that's over and done with now, right?" She made an effort to smile at him, but she was sad. He too twisted his face into a half smile, and thought, let her go and pull the wool over somebody else's eyes. That Israeli accent is only a disguise. She's one hundred percent American already. You can tell by that forced smile, those translated expressions, and the automatic way she tries to make conversation. Look how nice she was to that Asiatic parking lot attendant, what was he, Japanese, Chinese, maybe Vietnamese? She told him to have a nice day, with that pseudo-familiarity that is incomprehensible to anyone who isn't an American, and he called her Ma'am.

Bahat calmed down and began to feel satisfied on the whole. Things were coming along. She had found him at the airport, and he was now in her hands. Despite the beauty of the place, it wasn't every day that a scientist of such standing came to visit her in Ithaca, an Israeli what's more, and Bahat McPhee was ready to do *a lot* for him. For one thing, he had won the Israel Prize—which she would never win.

While studying to become a Reform rabbi, McPhee learned to hide her eccentricities, which had become very pronounced since her enforced loneliness. Over the years, ever since the exposure of the Emily Boston affair, her face had taken on an exaggeratedly severe expression, and she had become fanatical about noise. Even the singing of the birds at dawn disturbed her greatly.

Now she fell enthusiastically on the important guest and told him about her advanced studies in Judaism, but he wasn't interested. He nodded politely, but looked around at the sturdy maple trees. He immediately compared them to the coconut palm that had taken over the place where he lived. He wanted to tell McPhee about the palms of Tel Baruch North, but was unable to interrupt the torrent of her words, that were coming down on him now like an avalanche.

"He's really something, this masseur," she said suddenly, "By the way, he is also the president's masseur."

"Which president?"

"The President of the United States of America. By the way, the president is a graduate of our Cornell University, and not of Yale like everybody thinks. I'm taking you to him."

"To the president?" asked Gruber with some surprise.

"No," chuckled Bahat, "to his masseur from his student days, who has continued to remain close to him. He's first-rate. He'll put you on your feet in a minute."

For a while they drove in silence until her cell phone began to signal a text message.

"Must be one of my daughters," she said. "They really love me. This way we keep in touch all day long, even when they're in college. I'm very attached to them."

"I'm sure," mumbled Gruber.

She switched on the light in the car and tried to focus her eyes on the letters while driving.

"Read me what's written there," she asked in the end and handed him her cell phone.

"'Mother, I love you,'" he said. "But in English."

"Ah," sighed Bahat. "Don't tell me, it's the eldest. A treasure. But she wants to apply to Columbia University. I don't understand it. Why run to New York when you've got the best university in the world right next door?"

"It's a matter of adolescence," said Gruber, under duress, "my eldest is living in the Negev with some idiot, her boyfriend."

"Is that so?" Bahat was pleased. In Israel too children put a distance between themselves and their parents, you couldn't do anything about it, it was a law of nature.

8

FORTY MINUTES AFTER LANDING IN ITHACA, A PLACE IN which he had never set foot before, Gruber was lying in his underpants on the bed in the aromatic treatment room of the masseur of the incumbent President of the United States of America. Before burying his face in the pillow with a round hole that made it possible to breathe without effort, he managed to read the sign in English in a color that was a little too Indian for his taste. Something in the style of Lirit's clothes since she began going round with that creature. He read, "Leave the world, forget everything, let yourself rest," and thought that he had better do as it said.

"How do you want it?" asked the professional. "Strong Swedish?"

"Strong, yes, yes," said the Israeli. And he joked to himself: *Ha ha ha.* "Swedish . . ." he muttered aloud, and remembered that he was abroad and said, "Well done" in English.

In his own country Irad never let a week pass without retaining the services of one of the better masseurs in the Tel Aviv area, with a preference for Oren Berger, who was also the Israeli triathlon champion. A few of the residents of Bat Miriam Street had seen him on television. The guy would drive up on his Harley Davidson from his inferior neighborhood, making a terrible racket as if he didn't give a damn for Tel Baruch North, as if the whole thing meant nothing to him, as if he would never in his life live in one of the apartments there.

No more than twenty-five years old, he was already the Israeli triathlon champion and had been for three years in succession. With his youth and his motorbike that his parents had bought him after winning the title one autumn day that may have been dreary for many others, but was not for him— he felt like a king. A masseur who looked like a wrestler. Making house calls equipped with a special mattress and ethereal oils, he would spend the whole day in Tel Baruch North.

Gruber thought that the masseur he knew at home contained a contradiction: on the one hand, the Harley Davidson, an Israeli triathlon champion, the rough appearance with the tattoos and piercings, and on the other hand, a masseur with the most gentle touch in the Levant. All in one person: Oren Berger.

Mandy preferred hot stones on her once-beautiful back. It was not some proven scientific preference. Simply, she was so ashamed of herself for being sexually attracted to the Israeli triathlon champion. She calculated that he was six years older than her son, and this closeness in age embarrassed her greatly.

She really loved winners. Ever since she was twelve years old and her mother threw a bat mitzvah party for her in a hall in Dizengoff Street, close to where they lived on Arlozorov Street.

But Mandy had eyes in her head. She had received a very conservative education, and it was in her bones. As a woman pushing fifty, she knew that instead of letting Berger feel her body she should keep a safe distance from him, full of hot stones. Gruber talked a lot about the contradiction in the personality of the masseur, the Israeli triathlon champion, and it made her blood boil, but she didn't say anything, and only asked herself how many more times she would have to hear about the marvelous duality in this interesting person's personality.

Oren Berger, the dualist, wasn't crazy about the new neighborhood that had gone up almost overnight, but he had big ambitions to be both an internist and an acupuncturist and a doctor of Chinese medicine, and he needed a lot of patience. He had patience and motivation.

He would begin his rounds in Telba-N. on the corner of Yocheved Bat Miriam and Alexander Penn Street, and go on from there, to all the new streets which were almost all named after poets and writers of Hebrew and Jewish litera-ture. According to what he had found out, they were all big guns in poetry and literature and they were all dead. In the street named after Stefan Zweig, which he found on Google, he had two clients in almost every building, and it was a rela-tively long street.

On Fridays he would do his weekly round there, and then, at about five, he would go home and shower. On Saturday he would go out with his girlfriend to conquer the Judean Desert on his motorcycle. He never went over sixty miles per hour, even though he could. He could do up to two hundred and twenty, but he didn't like the resistance from the air.

Gruber thought a lot about Oren Berger, he actually forced himself to study this Baroque character. Sometimes, when Berger was giving him a massage and loosening the knots in his muscles, Gruber thought how lucky he was to have won the Israel Prize, and that he didn't have to run and swim and cycle for kilometers to do so (Gruber didn't know how to ride a bicycle, and at the age of fifty it was a little late to learn, never mind all that bullshit about how it's never too late). At the same time, he envied the young man for his amazing body.

He compared their two statuses and thought that they were more or less on a par, except that people would never call Gruber the *past* winner of the Israel prize, which gave him an advantage. He would never lose the title or the prize. In this sense he felt like the Frank Sinatra of Israeli science.

Oren Berger was never bored with Gruber. He felt close to Gruber, admired his quick thinking, and thought that to *him* Gruber could really talk, perhaps because they had both done something for the State of Israel. Therefore he felt it was legitimate to talk to the scientist about whatever was on his mind, and sometimes he would embark on long monologues about his exploits with his biker friends in the desert. Berger and his friends met every Saturday and rode to all the craters they felt like, as if Israel was full of craters.

Once Gruber had even asked him to stop bragging about his amazing life as a twenty-five year old.

A guy who on the previous Saturday had been to the ruins of a Nabatean city, and who had been there the Saturday before that too—how great was that?

By the way, the idea of implanting artificial shoulder blades came to Amanda Gruber from Oren Berger, who in the course of the two massages he had given her before she changed to the hot stones, told her about three of his clients, two white-collar and one from King George Street in Tel Aviv, women whose posture had been transformed by the operation. The one from King George Street walked round the city center with a bare back, proud of the carved peaks of her shoulder blades. It was actually through this woman that Mandy had reached Dr. Carmi Yagoda.

THE CURRENT MASSEUR made mincemeat of Oren Berger. With all due respect, Oren Berger might be a triathlon champion, but this guy was the champ of champs. The Yankee, who looked to be about Gruber's age, was so outstanding that the scientist soon stopped feeling the wound gaping in his heart ever since the collapse of his T-suit experiment. At last he let go of his personal Titanic and saw things in a general, cosmic, calming light.

"Lavender or sage?" asked the masseur.

"Excuse me?"

"Aroma in the room. Lavender or sage?"

"Sage," said Gruber to the annoyance of the masseur, who hoped he would go for lavender. Obediently he lit candles and dripped sage oil on the burner.

The American masseur, whose nickname was Hamlet, had majored in comparative literature at Cornell and graduated with honors. His diploma hung on the wall within sight of the treatment bed.

On the opposite wall the visitor from Tel Baruch North made out certificates for the completion of courses in massage and further studies in the field. Three of the diplomas were in Chinese or Japanese.

A third wall was full of hand-shaped *hamsa* amulets. Gruber estimated their number at about fifty, and he asked Hamlet if he believed in the Evil Eye. Hamlet replied that things often happened in his life which could be attributed to the Evil Eye that someone had given him. Gruber wanted to know if there was a connection between the number of amulets and the amount of bad energy sent him by envious people, and Hamlet said yes, but that was not the reason he kept dozens of amulets on the wall. He was simply keeping them for a very high up person.

"Who?" asked Gruber, and Hamlet ignored the impertinent prying and replied: "The president."

"The incumbent?" asked Gruber.

"Yes," said Hamlet without hesitation. "Every time he gets a *hamsa* from someone in your part of the world, he entrusts it to me. Who knows, maybe one day he'll have to leave the White House and return to Texas, and then he can take these amulets as a souvenir, and what's the harm if they incidentally also ward off evil eyes?"

They both fell silent. Hamlet kneaded Gruber's upper back and said: "Jesus, this isn't a back, it's concrete. Don't you have masseurs in the Middle East?" he asked, completely serious.

"Of course we do," said Irad Gruber in an insulted tone, "I simply had crazy flights that destroyed my back, and I'm under stress. The stress is killing me," he added, even though he was beginning to relax.

"Okay," said Hamlet and poured almond oil into his palms. "You'll walk out of here soft as a ripe tomato. Do you like tomatoes?"

"Very much," said Gruber.

"Which kind do you like better? The big ones or the small ones? Do you have the small ones?"

"Yes."

"Small round ones or small long ones?"

"Both kinds, I guess," he didn't like talking in English, and fell silent, apart from grunts of pleasurable and important pain.

And then came the really painful moment. Suddenly, something in his back! He screamed uninhibitedly. Hamlet recoiled.

"GOOD," said Hamlet regretfully. "They say that over here the taste is less natural, but I don't know the natural taste, so what do I care."

"What are you talking about?" asked Gruber, his whole back still hurting.

"The small round tomatoes."

Gruber couldn't stand the peace of mind that masseurs tried to convey. It annoyed him to be spoken to as if he was in a monastery.

"One of the times the president was here he brought me a divine basket of fruit."

He went back to work, concentrating on another area of the back, massaging and oiling, massaging and oiling, he too grunting.

"The president's got a lot on his mind now and I respect him. He has the elections to worry about. Otherwise he would get to Cornell more often. He really likes visiting his friends. A great guy. He'll win the elections.

"And now relax as if you're in a crater on Venus," he said slowly, in a low voice.

"What?"

"I took a little survey among my clients. What most relaxes them is a crater on Venus, or some other deserted planet, where the force of gravity is greater than on Earth.

And to imagine that nobody can see them. In this way they're forced to blot me out too, and causality, and judgmental attitudes, and I can tell you it relaxes most of them. Even though I'm married to a wonderful woman, before I go to sleep even I imagine that I'm alone on a deserted planet, and that I have no history. History is a load. A burden. Comparative literature is a burden too. A lot of things to remember. And so I decided to devote my life to my peace of mind."

"Ah, ah," Gruber groaned enjoyably as the latter smeared more oil on his back.

The masseur smiled to himself, sweating and satisfied, and said, "In half an hour tell me if you're ready to sign the wall behind you, which you can't see," and he turned his head to indicate it. "A wall of important, satisfied clients. Abba Eban signed it too. I liked the late Abba Eban a lot."

"If Abba Eban signed, I'll sign too," said Gruber without betraying his surprise. Even though he hadn't yet decided who it would flatter more, him or the former foreign minister.

"The former president of France, Georges Pompidou, signed too. Remember him?"

"How old are you?" Gruber suddenly asked. He himself hardly remembered the late Pompidou, and when he tried to imagine his face he wasn't sure that he wasn't confusing him with some other European leader. An Englishman maybe, or the secretary general of the United Nations.

"Fifty-nine," said the masseur.

"You should come and give massages in Israel," said Gruber.

For ten seconds, the masseur dragged out his chuckle at Gruber's joke—leave Ithaca to go and massage Israelis' backs!

"That's how it is with you people in the Middle East,"

he spoke again, after an interval, while massaging Gruber's scalp. "You kill them, they kill you. You have no choice, you have to kill one another," and he permitted himself to press down lightly on a few meridians.

"That's all," he said in his gentle voice, and went to the end of the room to wash his hands in the sink. Gruber noticed that he exaggerated his ablutions. While soaping and scrubbing his arms up to the elbows, Hamlet called out to him, "Get up very slowly without straining your neck. You have a problem with the first vertebra, which holds up the head. When you get back home, go and have an x-ray. I didn't work on it much, only around it, on the muscles."

He dried his arms on a towel that matched the other colors in the room: pale peach and magnolia.

"Get dressed behind the screen, you'll have time to think about signing the wall while you do it."

Irad got up slowly. The pain in his back was gone.

From behind the screen he heard Hamlet say, "The effect of the massage lasts for a few hours. You may feel tired."

"I'm tired anyway," said Gruber.

When he looked at the signature wall, he saw that they were all in Latin letters, except for Abba Eban's, who had signed in Hebrew. *A. Eban.* He signed in Hebrew next to him: *I. Gruber.*

IN THE BRIGHTLY LIT reception room, lacking any aroma of medicinal herbs, the Israeli scientist was about to pay for the enjoyable massage himself, but he was informed that Bahat had paid in advance.

Hamlet emerged from the treatment room with a pair of tongs holding a hot towel, which he wrapped round Gruber's neck, and said, "Run to Mrs. McPhee's car, the cold is bad for you. I've already called her."

The woman who was going to get his TESU project off the ground, and bestow eternal significance on his signature emblazoned next to that of Abba Eban, stepped out of her warm car with the engine still running to meet him, and quickly opened the door of the passenger seat. She smiled at him. Her teeth were as white as a toothpaste commercial.

"Thank you very much," he said.

"Don't mention it," she replied, and they drove off.

PART II

1

MANDY'S SHOULDER BLADE TRANSPLANTS, WHICH DIDN'T look bad at all, stuck out of the Medical Frontline blanket. It was clear that the operation had succeeded in principle, but she was in excruciating pain such as she had never felt in her life before. Not even after the liposuction from her stomach, which was considered complicated from the point of view of rehabilitation.

In the day that had passed since the surgery, Mandy had been blasted sky-high with pain and painkillers, from Voltaren to Percocet. She felt as if a world war was being fought within her.

She couldn't believe that this was happening to her, and she longed for the presence of one of her children to hold her hand and feed her water with a teaspoon, since she was lying on her stomach and couldn't drink anything without spilling it.

But one of them was in the army and the other was keeping an eye on the factory, and her husband was in America with some woman.

It was clear that something mythological was happening. Mandy Gruber, born in Rhodesia, resident of Telba-N., was not made for such levels of suffering. And not only the pain. The humiliation too.

"Nurse, nurse," she moaned.

Nobody answered.

She wanted morphine!

"Nurse! Nurse!" she tried again, in vain.

With a supreme effort, Amanda succeeded in reaching her cell phone (just how isn't clear, since she wasn't supple, her strong suit was aerobics—she had a class twice a week at the St. Tropez Institute in the Mikado complex) and dialed 144 to ask for the Medical Frontline number, in order to reach the ward in which she herself was hospitalized.

Someone said, "Inquiries 144, Hello. Adina speaking . . ."

Mandy was relieved not to have to remember the number they gave her but only to punch the star. She did punch the number of the extension for the recovery unit, heavily, and listened to seven long rings, which she heard, without synchronization, from the phone and also from behind the wall.

Usually Mandy had a very authoritative voice. She used it when she was giving motivational talks to the girls at the pajama factory. Once every few months Mandy asked Carmela to assemble them all in the neglected yard, and when they were standing in a semicircle, she herself stood on a step (you had to have a bit of hierarchy) and shot words at them.

During these talks Mandy felt at her best, and after them she was exhausted, sometimes she even went straight home.

"Come here at once!" she ordered the nurse who answered at last, but instead of the familiar authoritative tones she heard her voice petering out from one syllable to the next.

"Morphine," Mandy greeted the nurse who arrived all nice and friendly.

"You need the doctor's authorization," said the nurse.

"So ask for it," whispered Mandy.

"I'll ask, but I can tell you right now he won't agree to give you morphine on any account."

"That's . . . all . . . I . . . need," Mandy tried not to scream, but in the end she let out a loud scream, and even the nurse looked sorry for her.

"Okay, okay, I'll talk to him," she said.

Tears fell from Mandy's eyes. She bit her lip and waited for salvation to arrive.

Ten minutes later the nurse returned with the doctor on duty, a young man who had recently completed his residency and had an earring in his ear and a tag on his lapel that read "Dr. Bialystotski."

The nurse switched on the reading lamp. Mandy explained that she couldn't stand the pain. Dr. Bialystotski said, "That shouldn't be happening, let's examine you," and closed the curtains round her bed even though it was a private room.

ON ONE SIDE of the bed stood the nurse, on the other the doctor, and both of them together lifted the blanket with the sheet beneath it, and exposed the bandaged back. Then together they removed the bandages, and the young doctor very carefully, but nevertheless painfully, removed the sterile strips supporting the implants, touched here and there, and accompanied the touches with questions:

"Does it hurt here? Does it hurt here? Does it hurt here? And here?"

Mandy answered yes to every touch.

He asked, "Mrs. Gruber, are you sensitive to antibiotics?"

"No," she groaned.

"How much do you weigh?"

"Fifty-five kilo," she replied weakly.

He spoke to the nurse in terms of drugs and ccs. And there was a note of urgency in his words.

"And what about the morphine?" asked Mandy.

"Give her morphine," he instructed the nurse, with a severe expression on his face, "and first come with me to the office."

But he didn't wait until they reached the office. Mandy heard him raising his voice in the corridor.

"I don't like it. We have to locate that butcher from Dresden, Yagoda, immediately, and bring him back urgently. This surgery is his responsibility."

"But it's night now in Dresden too," said the nurse.

"I don't give a damn," he yelled, and sounded as if he had given himself a fright.

"Aah," he cried suddenly, "she has to be given a pulse of steroids immediately, and make an appointment for a bone-marrow test on Medical On Line for today! And don't forget Dr. Yagoda," his voice receded, as if he was talking to her while walking backward, "Keep at it until he answers the phone. Night time in Germany . . ." he snorted in contempt.

Mandy lay with her eyes closed, beside herself with suspense. The nurse came in and added something to the infusion.

"Is my condition grave?" asked Mandy.

"Grave? I wouldn't say so. Your condition is worrying, and it's being taken care of. Don't worry, the painkiller will help you in a minute. Think positive thoughts and good things will happen."

"Who can think at all?" asked Mandy, and the nurse didn't answer her.

IT WAS NOT ONLY avoiding thoughts of home that helped the good sniper to carry out his mission as he lay on the roof of a building in Tulkarem. It was not only the disconnection from his mother, that not thinking about her constituted a kind of rest for him. Sniper number two, Hai-Ad Gonen, had given him a bit of cocaine earlier, and Dael could already feel its blessed effects.

Dael Gruber, who all the guys in the army and in civilian life called Gruber due to the difficulty in pronouncing the two vowels one after the other, was regarded by his friends as a sensitive sniper with a delicate soul. And indeed, he was an example to contradict what people generally say about snipers in armies, that they detach themselves from feelings and simply say to themselves, "Someone has to do the job," and execute their task with cold-blooded composure. This was a sweeping generalization, and it didn't apply to Dael.

Dael went for it in a big way, in other words he shot to kill, otherwise it wouldn't have worked for him. It's a question of psychological makeup. Sometimes it was a little hard for him to shoot at a concrete target, but then he concentrated and took targets from his life instead and set them up in his imagination in the place of the wanted man. In many cases he imagined the father of Moran Eliot, his girlfriend when he was at the end of the eleventh grade, when she was at the end of the twelfth grade.

Moran Eliot was his first love. It lasted for June–July–August and half of September. Moran was his first, but he wasn't her first, and she said that after the first it didn't matter anymore what number he was. It ended badly between them, and with hindsight he didn't care. Her father was in his sights because he threw Dael out of the house in the most humiliating way, after Moran didn't want to see him and called him a stalker.

With Aya Ben-Yaish things were steadier, if with less fire. She was a spoiled kid who had moved to Tel Baruch North with her parents when her father had been obliged to sell their villa after going bankrupt, and rent an apartment in Telba-N.

They met for the first time in Mikado. She went down there in very short white pants, as dictated by fashion, to buy Winston Lights for her father, and Dael went to buy Winston Lights for himself. He smoked, of course. No great love erupted between them, but there was definitely a certain love, more meaningful than a convenient arrangement. However, it was true that the distance between Stefan Zweig Street, where the Ben-Yaish family lived, and Yocheved Bat-Miriam Street, where the Gruber family lived, was conveniently short, and Aya herself was pleasant and compliant on the whole.

IT WAS A RESERVIST psychologist in civvies who taught the snipers imaging. He arrived in the framework of a training course organized by the army for elite soldiers, and tried, for example, to explain what happened in the brain of the sniper at the time of shooting. He also gave advice on what to do in all kinds of specific stress situations within a general situation of stress. He divided their time according to levels of stress: very, very stressed, very stressed, and so on, down to apathetic. Dael and three other guys were the only ones who wrote down what he said, and so he spoke only to them, but mainly to Dael.

Dael also asked good questions, and the reservist was happy to answer them, and before answering each question he said, "I'm happy to answer your question."

He worked with them on controlling their emotions from the moment they left the base until they reached the site of the assignment. And then during the assignment until the minute they left the field. Dael wrote down all the tips, and looked at his bored companions and wondered what was going on in their heads. He imagined that what was going on it their heads was what would be going on in his head if he hadn't been so stressed by nature and had not lived in a house where stress was what connected the inhabitants.

The reservist gave them exercises for the suppression of irrational thoughts, and flavored his words with amazing stories about his own past as a senior sniper, before he became a psychologist, and Dael thought he was definitely okay, this guy, like his mother said about the friends he brought home. On principle, he told them to aim in their imagination at people they didn't feel anything in particular for, neither hate nor love. What he most recommended was a faint revulsion, and he confessed that he hit his own bulls eyes best when he imagined targets that aroused a faint revulsion in him, like teachers in high school, or even commanding officers in the army.

Dael thought that he could try, for example, the guests at his bar mitzvah. Not the ones that came to the synagogue, but the ones that turned up in droves after the service to lunch at the Stefan Baron restaurant.

But when none of the imaging exercises worked, and destructive thoughts swarmed into his mind like locusts, he thought about his father.

His hatred for his father was classic. His adoration of his mother was classic too. And his attitude toward his sister vacillated according to his mother's attitude toward her. In the days of Lirit's forbidden love for Lucas, sixteen-year-old Dael was the chief instigator of the family hostility toward the wayward girl, and on one particularly cold Saturday, when nobody wanted to leave their previous family home in Tagore Street, he wrote on the door of her room "Lirit the Parakeet," a nickname that had the power to insult her when she was a child, and to which she was still, at the age of almost twenty, not immune.

None of the family tried to defend Lirit. Their father, as usual, was absorbed in himself, and Mandy said that she had a bad case of the flu.

"THEY WANT TO HIT at the heart of the civilian population, because they know that this is where it hurts the nation most," the CO told them before the mission, but Dael thought that most of the nation didn't feel a thing, except perhaps for a faint pang, and because of this he needed a bit of cocaine before they set out: in order to hide the lie from his thoughts.

In that early spring simultaneity became a weapon in the ongoing war. The terrorist organizations competed among themselves as to how many simultaneous attacks they could mount, and every organization had a virtuoso who orchestrated the simultaneity.

The semi-senior wanted man Dael's force was assigned to liquidate was the virtuoso of the Fatah Eagles, a genius in his field, who according to the intelligence in the hands of the army, was busy planning five simultaneous attacks in different cities, including overseas targets. If the five bombs didn't explode at exactly the same minute, the attack wouldn't count as simultaneous. The number of casualties wasn't important, but the simultaneity was. The competition was over the control of time.

Where the five bombs were supposed to go off the intelligence agencies had been unable to discover, but the CO said in the briefing that he himself wasn't interested in knowing because in any case the planner would be eliminated today and he wouldn't be able to execute his plan.

YOU NEVER KNEW exactly when the shot would be fired. That was how the M24 sniper rifle was designed—in order to prevent the body's reflexes that could interfere with the execution of the execution. Dael compared the slow squeezing of the trigger to engaging the clutch on an uphill spurt, slowly, carefully, so the engine wouldn't stall. He had passed the test on his first go and he was an excellent driver. His mother let him have her fragrant car with an almost easy heart.

The lookouts confirmed that the target had been eliminated, together with its intentions to develop itself into five simultaneous explosions, including targets overseas. As for the force, it was already close to base. Dael's pulse was rapid, he was shaking and he wanted more cocaine. He sniffed his hands and cursed. Now his hands would stink for a week.

As usual afterward, he scrubbed himself for an hour in the shower and then lay down in bed and connected to the place where he had last stopped reading *The Red and the Black* by Stendhal. He allowed himself three pages before moving on to David Vogel. He had ten bookmarks, which Lirit had bought him for his nineteenth birthday, together with this book and another one by Jack Kerouac that was on sale. Was his simultaneous reading an obsession requiring treatment, or was it simply virtuosity, ostensibly superfluous? He remembered that his mother had told him a bookshop opened in Mikado and he wondered if they kept classics, or just the latest best sellers.

2

"WHAT?" ASKED GRUBER, WHO AFTER THE MASSAGE WAS ready both physically and mentally for a sleep of at least ten hours. "A French restaurant? Now?"

"Not just any French restaurant. Rene's Restaurant," said Bahat McPhee proudly.

Gruber yawned.

"I'm not hungry."

"I've already reserved a table. You have to make a booking there at least a week in advance, if we don't go now we'll never be able to go."

He stared at her, red eyed. Bahat felt guilty.

"Don't worry, it's a fantastic place, once you're there you won't want to leave," she said and drove too fast on the winding road.

"And we don't have to spend half the night there either," she said. "We won't stay more than two hours, but Rene's desserts are something special. You know he reopened the place just recently?"

"No," said Gruber.

"He had a restaurant that was doing very well, but he shut it down and went to France for a few years. And now he came back and opened it again, but in a different place. You know what, I've got something to cheer you up," she said and put on a tape.

Gruber couldn't believe his ears. Introductions to episodes of *The Twilight Zone*.

"In my opinion some of them are brilliant." She pressed stop, so she wouldn't have to go back after her explanations. "You know that Serling himself is the narrator in the series?"

"No," said Gruber in despair. In spite of the great massage, his neck could hardly hold itself up on his spine. If he had been condemned to death by the guillotine, his head would have come off even before the blade had finished its work.

"Listen," said Bahat and increased the volume to a disturbing degree.

You are traveling through another dimension, a dimension not only of sight and sound, but of mind.

Gruber looked at her in horror. Did she really intend playing him the introductions to all the episodes? How far was Rene's restaurant?

A journey into a wondrous land whose boundaries are that of imagination. That's the signpost up ahead—your next stop, The Twilight Zone!

She pressed stop and said: "Amazing, isn't it? The man was a genius. I don't think he's been given the credit he deserves. There's a whole society devoted to commemorating him. There was a time when I thought of joining, but it involved going to meetings with other people who admire him and his work . . ." She fell silent. "I don't like rubbing shoulders with people who only have one subject of conversation. It makes me nervous . . . He was a great artist. Have I already told you that he was a lecturer in communications at Ithaca College, and that my daughters studied there too?"

"Yes you have," said Gruber without remembering if she had or not.

They went on driving through a forest of tall thin trees. The darkness was absolute. Gruber couldn't understand how she allowed herself to drive at a speed of ninety miles per hour.

"A friend of mine from Berkeley taped these prologues for me."

"Very nice."

"It really was very nice of him. I told him so too. And it was from him that I heard about the Serling commemoration fund. He drew my attention to the fact that for only seventeen dollars you can get a really neat email address. Your name and then @rodserling.com. He himself has an address like that. But I think it's going a bit too far."

"So do I," said Gruber.

"But Raffi Propheta doesn't think so. His admiration of Serling knows no bounds."

"Who's Raffi Propheta?" asked Gruber, and for a moment he was afraid he had missed something important.

"My friend. From Berkeley University. He made this tape for me. He teaches Hebrew at Berkeley, and he's active in the Serling commemoration fund. He's a very special person. From the moment I heard that he too was a Serling fan he shot up in my estimation. He lives in Berkeley. I never visit him. Not because I've got anything against Berkeley, but because I simply can't leave the spiders for long. It's enough that I go to the Hebrew Union College in New York. It really makes me nervous to leave the spiders, even though since they stuck me with the Hispanic I'm less nervous about leaving the research without supervision."

"Clearly."

"My relations with Raffi Propheta are platonic, there's nothing between us except for conversations in Hebrew. He's the only person I know here who I can speak Hebrew to the way I'm speaking to you. Naturally I can find Israeli students in Ithaca, the place is full of them, by the way, but talking to students isn't much fun. Apart from which, he's up to date on all the changes in Hebrew slang, and he has a student who's doing a doctorate in the subject under his supervision. They've got a lot of respect for him in Berkeley. You've never heard of him in Israel? Raffi Propheta?"

"It's not my field."

"Right," she giggled. Gruber noticed that she was familiar with all the turns in the winding road and took them automatically.

"I had a serious moral problem with him, but I overcame it. All in all I learned a lot about Rod Serling from him. For example, that he comes from a Jewish Reform family, and that he became a member of the Unitarian church, and also that he was a boxer. Did you know that?"

"No," admitted Gruber.

"Serling made a movie called *Heavyweight Requiem*. He was a Renaissance man. He was a paratrooper too. He served in the US army and fought like a hero."

"Good."

"And he was only five foot three."

"Is he dead?"

"He died in seventy-five. But before that he collected six Emmy awards," she added proudly.

Gruber's mental condition was desperate. He was convinced that he was being driven by a woman who was not right in her head. But at the same time he knew that this did not contradict the fact that she had the ability to help him in his limping research.

"He's pro-Arab and anti-Israel big time," she said as if revealing a great secret.

"Who?"

"Propheta. Whenever the IDF kill someone he calls and barks at me as if I'm the virtuoso mind behind the army's activities in the territories."

"Obviously not," said Gruber.

"But I need him," she said in the tone of an intimate confession. "I need to speak Hebrew on the phone or face to face. I'm not sexually attracted to him, you mustn't think . . . the fact that he hates Israel makes it impossible for me to see him in that light. I like him, but not that much. Listen to this, in my opinion this is one of the best introductions—"

Again Serling's voice filled the interior of the car:

There is a fifth dimension beyond that
which is known to man.

"Are you listening?"

"Yes, yes," Gruber made haste to reply.

It is a dimension as vast as space and as timeless as
infinity.

119

"If there's a word you don't understand tell me."
"I understand."

It is the middle ground . . .

"The halfway point," shouted McPhee.

. . . between light and shadow, between science and superstition, and it lies between the pit of man's fears and the summit of his knowledge. This is . . .

Gruber noticed that she was moving her lips together with the tape, and he felt a great sense of detachment.

. . . the dimension of imagination. It is an area we call the Twilight Zone.

"My pro-Arab friend from Berkeley has all the episodes that come after these introductions on DVD. Would you like me to get them for you?"
"No, no. We have the same thing in Tel Aviv too."
"Okay," she said in disappointment. "I only wanted to help. You know that I only want to help," she said and gave him a meaningful look, that lasted too long for someone who should have been keeping her eyes on the road. And then she returned her eyes to the road and they drove for a while in silence until she stopped the car, put on the hand brakes, and said in a childish voice, "Here we are."

Gruber saw a depressing three-storied building. In darkness.

His sense of strangeness instantly deepened and he

felt dizzy too, as if his whole body was suddenly operating according to different laws of physics, those of a kind of Twilight Zone. This Israeli woman from the arthropod forum was bringing him to an abandoned building, that she claimed was a fancy French restaurant. With all due respect, he was not yet ready to explore another dimension.

"Come along," said Bahat, and they both got out of the car, which she locked with a screech of the alarm.

"The entrance is round the other side. Careful how you go. The stones are slippery here from the deluge that came down before you landed. Did you feel it on the plane?"

He didn't answer, only walked behind her in the dark. They entered the building. Bahat said, "It was once a geriatric hospital."

They walked down a long corridor, on the right and left were peeling green doors with numbers on them, 212, 213 . . .

"A French restaurant in a hospital?"

"The hospital isn't operating, the restaurant is," said Bahat and opened a brown door, revealing a dimly lit French restaurant full of diners.

"Name please?" a hostess pounced on them.

"McPhee," said McPhee, and took off her coat, helped Gruber off with his, and handed them both to the hostess.

McPhee smiled at Gruber, and he thought the smile was false and that her teeth were as white as those of a lot of Americans. But he also thought that when he got back to Israel he would have his own teeth whitened, he was a public personality, winner of the Israel Prize, he couldn't afford to go round with plaque and yellow teeth.

The hostess led them to a table that did not meet with McPhee's approval, and she requested another table. There was no other table available, and she asked for Rene to be called. Rene arrived during the middle of a lovers' quarrel at one of the tables, and as a result a table to McPhee's taste becoming available. As soon as they sat down she said something she had planned to say before, but hadn't managed to:

"It's hard to know if there are more pro-Arabs than Arabs at Berkeley. In my opinion there are. But perhaps now it's balanced out a bit. After all, the pro-Arabs need Arabs next to them so that they can show them that they're on their side."

"Presumably," said Gruber and he looked at the menus and didn't understand a thing.

"I'll explain," said McPhee and she explained all the dishes to him.

Gruber looked at her and realized that never in all his life had he felt so alienated anywhere.

But perhaps it was only the tiredness, he tried to encourage himself, and decided to stop asking himself questions and to start taking an interest in the menu. Suddenly he felt hungry too, and he even said so to Bahat.

"I told you so, the appetite comes with the food."

Gruber didn't like having this kind of saying repeated to him. He worked out what time it was in Israel, and he felt like calling someone there now, never mind who, and suddenly he realized that he had forgotten his cell phone in Tel Baruch North, on the bedside table, for some reason on Mandy's side.

"Oy," he said sadly.

"What's wrong?"

"I forgot my cell phone at home," he said.

"Do you want mine? You want to make a call? What time is it over there?"

"What time is it over *here*?" He smiled. "No, never mind."

It seemed to him that he wouldn't be able to produce a single sentence in Hebrew now that would sound authentic. He was probably beginning to take on an American tinge himself, and whoever answered the phone in Israel would notice it at once, and conclude that Irad Gruber wasn't solid enough and that he changed in accordance with whatever country he happened to be in.

During the course of the meal, which lasted for exactly two hours, McPhee talked without stopping, only pausing when her mouth was full. Gruber ate and nodded, sometimes smiling and sometimes looking serious; there were even moments when he tried to engrave what he was eating on his memory, but his thoughts wandered. All his numbers were in his cell phone memory. If anything here was as it should be, and this woman had important and useful information, he would have to let the Defense Minister and the head of WIDA know immediately. How was he going to do that without the numbers on his cell phone? He was too tired to find a solution, and he ordered crème brûlée and decaffeinated espresso.

Bahat was drunk and asked him to drive back. All the way on the winding road between the forest of tall thin trees he thought about Rod Serling who had written about the beyond and the fifth dimension and the imagination, collected six Emmy awards, and died young.

3

IN ISRAEL THE DAY WAS COMING TO THE END OF THE TWI-
light hour, and all its beauty was going to be over in a matter of seconds. Lirit came home after an exhausting working
day at Nighty-Night, tanned as if she had spent two weeks in
Eilat. In fact, she had gone straight from the pajama factory
to the health club at Mikado, where she had obtained a spray-
on tan, and now she was suffering from a guilty conscience
for not going to see her mother all day. She imagined that
she wasn't doing too badly, and comforted herself with the
thought that tomorrow she would go before work.

The tan looked terrific, authentic and even, Lirit said to
herself as she examined her naked body in the mirror. Shlomi
was right not to like nudity with color differences left by
swimsuits. A swimsuit seemed to him an artificial additive.
Lirit thought that she would return to their home in Brosh
on the border of Te'ashur in two, maximum three days, and
at the health club they told her that the tan would last up to
a week.

Because of his views she made up her mind *not* to tell him
how she had acquired the tan, but to say that she had sun-
bathed in the nude on the roof of the pajama factory.

She called Medical Frontline and someone who didn't

actually have a clue told her that her mother was sleeping after receiving strong painkillers.

Now Lirit looked like a typical Telba-North girl of her age: blonde streaks—which someone like that would have done herself for a few dollars or at the Mikado hairdressing salon when she had the time—thin but not emaciated, quite tall, and most importantly self-confident beyond what you would expect for someone of her age, as if the majority of her achievements were already behind her, and all she had to do now was go from strength to strength. Most of the inhabitants of Tel Baruch North, even if they weren't twenty-two-year-old girls with blonde streaks, were self-confident to a fault. It may well be that the evergreen vegetation, together with the slightly exaggerated resemblance of the houses, whether multistoried or not, had in the end done the job, whether the planners had planned it or not: they had implanted in the inhabitants what was so sorely missing in other suburbs of Tel Aviv, the conviction that the place would survive a war.

She didn't know if she was allowed to take a shower, and she called them to ask. They said yes she was, no problem. In the shower she felt flooded by pity for her mother, who had been buried for years in a place where there were only female workers, most of them ugly, and the only man who sometimes came there was the Singer technician, maybe the same one who had come onto her grandmother, and maybe also to the next generation.

Lirit dried herself quickly and took a big white T-shirt belonging to her father from the walk-in closet, put it on, lay down on her parents' comfortable bed, switched on the remote of the plasma screen television, which was a little too big for the size of the room, and gave her the feeling that she was sitting in the front row of a movie theater.

She switched from the BBC World News to the Good Life Channel, but they were only showing cooking programs there, and Lirit wasn't really keen on the subject, especially since she was under no obligation to get to grips with it as yet. She switched to the E! Channel, to see the homes of celebrities residing in Hollywood.

All the homes of the celebrities were standing firmly on their foundations, and the celebrities were very happy with their homes and their careers, even though they had known ups and downs. They showed a singer who had gotten into trouble, and was now in danger of losing everything, including his personal freedom.

Lirit opened the drawer of her mother's bedside table and took out a bottle of Yves Saint Laurent pink nail polish, opened it, sniffed the smell she loved, and started to paint her toenails.

Her mother's business pink didn't really go with the rather savage orange-brown of her skin, but she couldn't find the remover. She waited for the nail polish to dry, and after that she didn't have any plans. Shlomi hadn't called or sent a text message, and she was very tense, to the extent of a pounding in her heart every two minutes. Beads of sweat stemming from the fear of abandonment, mixed with the fear of life without him, collected on her forehead. Lirit didn't admit to herself that she found Shlomi somewhat boring, and that therefore the fact that he hadn't called was enough to make him fascinating in the extreme.

On the movie channel *The Postman Always Rings Twice*

was starting, with her mother's favorite actress, Jessica Lange, and Lirit thought it was the right thing for today to watch a movie starring her mother's favorite actress.

All through the movie she was preoccupied by Shlomi's failure to call. If she had been alert to her feelings and in touch with them in real time, she would have demanded a clarification from Shlomi weeks ago, when the crack began. On the other had, it was clear what he would say. He would say again that you couldn't swim in the same river twice.

Shlomi got on Lirit's nerves with this proverb, and Lirit didn't know anymore if she loved *him*, really *him*, or if she was just obsessive about him and a junkie for his approval.

She examined her cell phone again. Perhaps in the meantime he had sent a text message, or a heart, or a smiley, but the cunning little screen was empty, and it only showed the time and the state of the reception and the battery, and it was all so empty! No picture of an envelope and no sign of a call that hadn't been answered, for example, when she was in the shower. She hardly had any incoming calls. Ever since she had gone down south, she had cut off all contact with her girlfriends.

She turned her eyes back to the plasma screen. She tried to remember the name of the male lead playing opposite Lange, but she couldn't, because she had never heard of him anyway.

She made up her mind to wait for the credits at the end of the movie and learn this missing detail.

Suddenly she noticed that she felt good. Comfortable. Secure. And that the only thought disturbing her peace of mind was that Shlomi hadn't called. If she dismissed this thought from the course of her life, at least for a while, everything would be all right.

There was no doubt that escaping from the natural and organic life with Shlomi to the artificial life supported by every possible gadget had done her good. All in all she had really missed civilization and especially globalization, and wanted to buy some Diesel clothes, and a few other brands that enriched the rich and impoverished the poor. She planned on a big shopping spree before going back south, and wondered if she should take her new acquisitions with her to Brosh on the border of Te'ashur, or leave them in Telba-North.

Fifteen minutes after the sensational sex on the kitchen table in *The Postman Always Rings Twice* her cell phone rang, and Lirit recognized Shomi's cell number on the screen, which meant that Shlomi was using it now in spite of his repudiation of all its upgraded features because a call from cell to cell cost less. Lirit let it go on ringing for her own enjoyment and she thought, there you are, as soon as you let go, he called.

She wanted to sound busy with something entirely different, like a person with a world and life of her own, of which Shlomi constituted only a small derivative even though she respected this derivative. At the same time she wanted to give her hello a happy note, because they were in a relationship after all, and why hide happiness if it existed. But already by the sound of Shlomi's hello she understood that they were in for a serious discussion of essential issues. She really didn't feel like starting this kind of discussion now, in the middle of the movie, and so she immediately adopted a despondent tone:

"My mother's not doing too well."

And thus she succeeded in forcing Shlomi to take an

interest in the health of her mother, who he couldn't stand anyway. Only after he had complied with the demands of common humanity, he turned to the personal: quite simply, he wanted to split up with Lirit. It was quite simple, he said again. He needed to live by himself for a while, it wasn't an absolute separation, but it was definitely a separation. Quiet detachment.

"Why?" she asked.

"I'm going through a very difficult period with myself," she heard him say. "I'm over forty, and I haven't achieved anything in my life. I haven't even got a house of my own. Or a profession. The world's getting harder and harder. I can't adjust to it and I ask myself why."

"And because the world's getting harder and harder you want to separate from me?" asked Lirit.

"Yes, Lirit. It doesn't suit me to be with you when I don't value myself. You deserve better. Tell me, what am I to you? An aging loser who hates what he has become. I have to take it in spite of the wound to my ego, and to think about what to do next."

"You're not a loser," said Lirit in a raised voice, but it didn't help her to suppress the thought that he actually was. Shlomi was a loser according to plenty of criteria, except perhaps for those related to Buddhism or Zen-Buddhism.

"I thought that with you far away in the north, it was an excellent opportunity to tell you what I'm going through," he said.

"Don't you love me anymore?" Lirit asked him glumly, since neither Shlomi's career nor his satisfaction with himself interested her, but only how he felt about her.

"I don't know what love is. I only know that you can't

swim in the same river twice and that what's past is past. If our relationship is to continue it has to be something new, and only after I know more about myself."

"And isn't it possible," the girl from Telba-North made bold to ask, "for me to be at your side while you think? I'm quite quiet," she said suddenly. "I won't disturb you, if that's what you're afraid of."

"No-no-no," pronounced Shlomi. "I'm not making it easy on myself. If I wanted to, I could go and stay with my mother in Sefad. I intend to stay here on my own and to break my head alone."

"Hey, that's a rhyme."

"It came out by accident," he said wearily.

There was an oppressive silence.

"Good," said Shlomi.

"Good," repeated Lirit.

"That's it'" said Shlomi.

"That's it?"

"That's how it is."

"Okay."

She hung up quickly because she didn't want him to hear her cry. True enough, the guy was broken down and boring. But if she lost him—what would she do then?

Loss suddenly broke into Lirit's life. Her mother had taught her that in situations that were impossible to bear, simply impossible, because the nightmare was larger than life, there was no alternative: you anesthetized yourself. At the moment it was clear to the former NCO-Casualties that she was stuck in a busy junction, without any traffic lights, not even blinking ones, and the situation was really scary. And so she detached herself from it.

She went to the medicine cabinet and found her mother's kits arranged in little bags of cocktails: a bag with five Clonex zero-point-fives and two Vabens of ten milligrams and a Bondormin or two. Another bag contained one Clonex of two milligrams and six Bondormins, without Vaben, and so on, about twenty little bags with cocktails for anesthetizing sensation, consciousness, personality, and the body that contained all the above.

She chose a cocktail that was more or less pure Clonex, with just one Bondormin, and calculated that when she woke up, she would be able to cope with the sudden emptiness in her life where being part of a couple used to be, but in the meantime she went to the handsome kitchen, filled a disposable glass with too-cold water from the mineral water container, and swallowed the cocktail with its help.

Afterward she closed all the electric blinds in the house, not God forbid in anger, but with the decisiveness of a woman doing something that had to be done, and returned to her parents' suite, which was as clean and tidy as a hotel suite because the Columbian cleaner had been there in the morning. First of all, she switched off her cell phone. Disconnected it completely, rather than putting it on mute, so that whoever called would get it in his face that the subscriber was *not available* and he should try again later. By this blunt treatment of the instrument she also denied herself the desire to look at the little screen and see how many calls—or, God forbid, what if none at all, which was also possible—had gone unanswered.

The young woman was well aware that the reality of her life was undergoing a process of change and that she had to get ready to deal with it differently. If Shlomi broke her

heart—something she was no longer so sure would happen—
she would cry only after she had taken care of her mother,
and after her father had returned to Israel, and after Dael had
survived the army, when life got more or less back on track,
or found a different track.

She got into her parents' beautiful comfortable bed, and
the pills she had taken put her to sleep in five minutes.

4

RITA, THE INTENSIVE CARE NURSE IN ICHILOV HOSPITAL, tried every possible means of contacting the family of the patient Amanda Gruber, who had arrived straight from Medical Frontline in critical condition.

She got the phone numbers from Amanda herself, but there was no answer from the patient's home, her daughter's cell phone announced immediately that the subscriber was not available, and her son's cell phone rang and rang to no effect.

Dael didn't answer because he didn't answer unidentified numbers on principle. His father, Irad Gruber, had instilled an aversion to unidentified numbers in him because all the numbers at WIDA were unidentified, apart from his own. Gruber preferred to remain identified, and thus to know if he was being screened.

While Rita was desperately calling him and his sister by turn, the outstanding sniper was busy on his base somewhere in the country, surfing the Internet by means of an upgraded cell phone belonging to a friend. He was searching for schools for paparazzi in the United States.

He found one in Santa Monica, one in Santa Barbara, one in Santa Fe, and one in Santa Cruz, and in another six places without Santas. He copied the addresses into a notebook where he wrote down sentences from important books. Only after repeated rings, when he could no longer overcome his curiosity to discover the identity of the insistent anonymous caller, he answered the phone.

And then—*go* wasn't the word. He shot like a missile to his CO, who commanded him to make for his mother pronto, and volunteered to drive him to the station in time to get the last train to Tel Aviv. From the CO's car he tried to get his sister at his parents' home, but there was no answer, and her cell phone was silent too.

He couldn't take the news that his mother was in critical condition single-handed, and he felt as if he was collapsing into himself.

While he was waiting for the train, he remembered his sister's number at Shlomi's, and when he called it, Shlomi answered, and Dael asked him if he had heard anything.

Shlomi had always been cool to him, because he thought that Dael had blood on his hands, that he was nothing short of a murderer, and that he should have refused to obey orders. This time Shlomi was really nasty, and only after Dael explained how grave the situation was, Shlomi volunteered the information that he had spoken to Lirit a few hours before, and added that since Dael was suddenly so worried about Lirit, he was beginning to feel worried too and asked Dael to keep him informed of further developments.

DAEL HAD NO INTENTION of keeping this schmuck informed about any developments. The loathing between them was mutual. It had come to a head one Friday night the previous winter when Shlomi had done them the favor of showing up at the apartment in Telba-North, after Lirit had pressured him into it. Mandy had prepared a relatively festive meal. Usually she bought takeout from selected delis, but this time she surpassed herself and made a quiche and salads—all organic, without pesticides, chemicals, and genetic modifications.

Around the table they talked about Dael's ambition to study to become a paparazzo abroad, and to photograph celebrities on the local scene in poses that up to now had never graced a camera. Shlomi argued that this was an invasion of privacy and Dael insisted that the minute someone was a celeb—his life was no longer his own business.

Lirit tried to change the subject, and asked those present if they had seen that a Michal Negrin boutique had been opened in Mikado. Mandy couldn't stand the jewelry they sold at those shops and shut her daughter up, without any sensitivity to the diversionary tactics her offspring was attempting to put into play, with the result that Shlomi launched into an inflammatory speech against Tel Baruch North and its inhabitants.

Dael remarked that with all due respect to the saying that fresh eyes see every flaw, Shlomi didn't know enough to form an opinion about any neighborhood North of the Yarkon River. But Shlomi insisted that it was enough to check out a few streets here in order to know what you were up against, and Dael replied (apparently in order to impress Aya Ben-Yaish, who was also present at the table, but who kept quiet, except for occasionally giggling shyly, or spitefully, who knows) that for someone who couldn't stand the place or the people who lived there, he couldn't seem to keep his hands off one of them, meaning Lirit.

Lirit and Mandy exchanged shocked looks. Irad Gruber didn't bat an eye, and only when Mandy whispered to him that his autism was off the charts, he intervened and said, "Okay-okay, enough-enough-enough, everybody shut up."

Later that evening, when they were putting the dishes in the dishwasher, one rinsing in the sink and the other arranging, the mother and daughter decided to refrain in future from inviting Shlomi and Dael to sit at the same table because there was an ideological chasm yawning between them. That same week Dael was sent on a mission to eliminate someone heavy, and he imagined Shlomi and hit right in the center of the wanted man's body mass.

ON THE TRAIN to Tel Aviv Dael tried his father's cell phone a few times too, but in the end he understood that perhaps he hadn't taken it with him to America at all.

The person sitting opposite him was sucking air through his teeth, as if an obstinate crumb was stuck there and he was trying to suck it out. The noise he was making with his teeth got on Dael's nerves, and he asked himself how he could approach him without insulting him. Every formulation that occurred to him was disqualified as soon as he imagined what he himself would feel if someone had addressed him in such a way in the middle of the train. He had a talent for stepping momentarily into somebody else's shoes, which ostensibly seemed completely in contradiction to the fact that he was also an outstanding shot. But he never stepped into the shoes of the people he shot.

He moved to another seat and rang home again and met again and again with the answering machine, which said in Mandy's voice, "You have reached the Gruber family: Amanda Gruber," (yes, she jumped to the head of the queue), "Irad Gruber, Lirit Gruber and Dael Gruber. You may leave a message for any of these."

Dael thought about the word "these." She could have said "them," or simply said nothing after the word "message," but Mandy, who had arrived in Israel at the age of eight, still had a complex about not being a sabra, and took every opportunity to display her mastery of the Hebrew language.

He couldn't understand what was happening to his sister. "Troubles never come singly," his mother liked to say, and added "God forbid." The possibility of his sister being in trouble horrified him, and he tried to remember the name of their neighbors, something like Rotterdam, but not actually Rotterdam . . . He recalled his mother saying that she had doubts about their Jewishness because of their Flemish appearance, and he remembered that their name was Amsterdam.

He called information and wrote down their number on the beautiful bookmark he took out of *The Red and the Black*. The doubtful neighbors were diligent but not at all efficient. They rang and rang, knocked and knocked, called, "Lirit, Lirit," but got no reply. They told Dael that they could hear the phone ringing in the triplex. Mr. Amsterdam suggested calling someone to break in, but Dael thanked him politely.

He put his gun down on the seat on his right, passed the strap over his head to his left shoulder, and buried his head in his hands.

He had never felt so guilty. If he hadn't been doing this job in the army, his mother wouldn't have gone in for plastic surgery and Lirit wouldn't have had to come up north in order to take charge of the factory.

He raised his head and looked at the approaching lights of Lydda and decided to prioritize. His mother was in certain danger, and he would therefore concentrate on her and set the mystery of Lirit aside for the time being.

AMANDA GRUBER PASSED AWAY at five fifty in the morning, Israel time. An hour before Dr. Yagoda left his home in Dresden in order to spend the following days and nights recuperating on the banks of some lake or other. In any case, there was nothing he could have done. A virulent germ had attacked the area of the operation. Usually this germ was friendly, but in rare cases it became virulent and consumed the bones rapidly.

Dr. Atzmon Lidani, the intensive care doctor, didn't tell Dael and Lirit (who, after she woke up, was located safe and sound at home) in so many words that their mother was turning into a boneless mollusk. They understood for themselves. Dr. Lidani only told the horrified children that the bacteria had attacked their mother at five different points, and that the stronger it became from devouring the bones the faster it worked. Dr. Lidani did all he could. The minute he admitted the patient to intensive care, he had drawn up a protocol of liquids for her and given her pulses of steroids and huge quantities of antibiotics. In the meantime he had located an international expert on the bacteria in question on the Internet, in the state of Virginia. He had found him on vacation in Miami, and proceeded according to his instructions.

"He's number one in the world, and I hold him in very high esteem," said Dr. Lidani to Mandy's children, "Let's pray that something takes."

"We'll cross our fingers," said Lirit.

Mandy was no stammerer, and even though she disliked the Hebrew language, she knew how to speak it fluently and very well. But now she had great difficulty in speaking since the bacteria had attacked the bones of her face and jaw.

"Nothing left," she said. "Not worth it. The elbows. The head. It's in the skull. Enough. No towels in the Sheraton. All finished."

Lirit couldn't bear to hear her mother talking like this, in sober despair and at the same time not to the point. The combination made her uncomfortable. She wanted to remember her at her best, and she told Dael that she was going to the vending machine to fetch hot chocolate for him and coffee for herself.

On her way back with the two brown plastic glasses, she heard her mother shouting, "Ohhhhhhh," threw both glasses out of the window in a panic, and ran into the room.

Mandy had succeeded in raising herself on her stomach (the condition of her spine gave her an unnatural flexibility) and she was pleading with Dael to tell the nurse to turn her onto her back.

"Morphine. Lots. And head up."

The nurses didn't dare turn her over on their own initiative and went to look for the doctor. Dr. Lidani gave his permission, on the grounds of human dignity. He gave instructions for her to be given a heavy dose of an extreme painkiller, to wait for it to take maximum effect, and then to turn her over with her face to the ceiling.

Dael and two nurses turned her over and fixed the pillows, and Mandy whispered:

"To die on my back. Not my stomach. At least."

It was apparent that she was gathering her strength. "Children. Body to science. The funeral later. For what's left. No to organic cotton." She looked at her horrified daughter. "No nonsense. My line to continue. Like my mother. From generation to generation." After it seemed that she had fallen silent, she added with a unique effort, "I'll haunt you from above."

"Yes, yes, mother," mumbled Lirit without believing her. She wondered if she would really haunt her, and remembered how her mother would say that death was the unraveling of a thread from the fabric of life, and from the point of view of the dead, death was a final exit. It seemed to Lirit that she had discovered a contradiction in her mother's words, because if death was a final exit, the unraveling of a thread, how would she be able to haunt her from above?

"Only the ultra-Orthodox market. Only them. No tricks," Mandy mumbled, and then she began to rattle, and the rest followed as usual, until death, the road to which was padded with generous amounts of morphine, because why let them suffer?

THE DOOR TO the Intensive Care Unit opened again to the brother and sister Gruber, this time on their way out.

"What time is it in the United States?" asked Lirit.

"Seven hours back."

"Back? Not forward?"

"Back."

"But there are a few time zones there. At least four."

Dael didn't answer because his world had collapsed. What did he care what time it was, even in Israel?

They walked silently down the vale of tears of the Ichilov corridors, until they reached the elevator.

The stock of the M24 got stuck between the two closing doors, and Dael groaned and pulled the gun toward him. He was still in uniform.

"I don't know what to do," he said, "I don't understand this situation."

Lirit led her brother in the direction of their mother's car, in which she had arrived. While she was racing into the Ichilov Hospital underground parking, she had muttered to herself, "What a terrible thing to happen . . . what a terrible thing to happen." And now, as she wandered round with her brother looking helplessly for the way out, she thought that it really was a catastrophe. She asked Dael:

"What's going to happen now?"

Dael didn't answer again, because his thoughts were a mess. When they arrived at the parking lot and it turned out that Lirit didn't actually remember where she had parked, because of course she was very upset, he said, "Find the car already. I'm dying to get out of here. There isn't enough oxygen here. They should hand out oxygen masks at the entrance to the parking garage, not a ticket. Did you pay?"

"No," she said, and by chance they found a pay station.

"Do you remember the color? The section?"

"Orange I think. Green. I don't know."

"Brilliant," he said.

They split up to look for the car in the oxygenless site.

Dael continued in minus two, and Lirit went down to minus four. In minus four there was even less oxygen, and judging by the suffocating atmosphere Lirit guessed that the car was on this level. And indeed she found it, got in and switched on the ignition, and drove up to minus two, where her brother was sitting on some step, after giving up his search.

"Come on," she called to him and opened the window of the seat to her right. "I found it."

Dael got up, threw his gun and bag onto the back seat, and sat down next to her.

"*Yallah*, let's get out of here," he said.

5

IRAD GRUBER SWITCHED ON THE TELEVISION SET OPPOSITE his bed. He had no idea what time it was, neither here nor in Israel. On the screen two men maligned one another refereed by the host. Probably a repeat broadcast. A televised debate between two presidential candidates. The incumbent Republican, his face flushed and his expression resolute, and the Democrat, his skin gray, his face long, his look beaten. Gruber tried to take sides in order to give himself an interest in the debate that had nothing to do with him, just as he sometimes did when watching a football game on TV. But he lacked sufficient data on the American scene, and after a few minutes he was sick of their talk and began to flip channels.

Couldn't be better! *All in the Family*—his favorite series of all time! And what's more, an episode he couldn't remember seeing when it first came out. Gruber smiled to himself when the familiar characters appeared on the screen, chuckled from time to time, and once even laughed out loud.

His laughter woke Bahat McPhee, who was sleeping in the next room. The laughter was uninhibited, carefree, not at all that of someone whose scientific world had come crashing down around him. She felt a little envious of the Israeli man who was capable of forgetting how grave his situation was.

She glanced at her watch. In another hour or two a pale light would dawn outside. Bahat detested the pale dawn light, a detestation dating from the period of her parents' yoga studio in the green suburb of Ramat Aviv. She thought that normal people should be sleeping when the sun began to rise because it had nothing to do with them. Sunrise! Sunset, maybe. It expressed a lot of feeling. But all this excitement over a pale, boring sunrise got on her nerves, with all due respect.

In the end she gave up and switched on the TV in her room and listened with interest to the debate, with her eyes closed because she had missed the live broadcast. She was divided in her mind over the elections. One of the candidates was good for Israel and not so great for the Americans, and about the other they said that the USA was his top priority and that he thought America should look inwardly. Despite all the years that had passed since she last set foot on the land of Israel, Bahat was unable to choose sides in light of such divided data.

BAHAT HAD LEFT Israel at the end of the seventies, and since then she had only returned for the funerals of her mother and father respectively, and had not even stayed till the end of the week of mourning. She was one of those Israelis who are reluctant to stay in Israel because of fear, especially since the nineties, and it was just about then she also fell under the spell of Rod Serling, something that had a big influence on the bedrock of her reality.

From the beginning of the third millennium, Israel already seemed to her as frightening as Iraq. Afula and Falluja, Karkur and Kirkuk, what was the difference, she would sometimes sit and muse in the morning, with her sixth coffee and cigarette.

Since acquiring the title of Reform rabbi was conditional on spending at least one full year in Israel, she decided, on the advice of and with the consent of the most respected female rabbi in the congregation of Albany, that she, Bahat McPhee, would instead make a great, pure gesture, one that called for charity and sacrifice, toward the state of Israel, and the Albany rabbi would exempt her from the obligation of staying there for a year.

Sacrifice and charity for the sake of Israel would stand to her credit long after she became a Reform rabbi too, and Bahat liked the idea of having an advantage over all the others; it was pathological with her, the desire to open a gap, but she had been this way since she was a child.

Bahat McPhee gave a lot of thought to the move she would make. Carefully she calculated what she would lose and what she would gain. In the period of enthusiasm preceding Gruber's arrival she became addicted to caffeine, and smoked like a Frenchwoman. And due to her smoking, her social problems grew more acute. Even before this nobody could have called her a popular personality in the Jewish community of Ithaca, or in the scientific community of Ithaca, or in the general population of Ithaca either. She had no status and/or charisma to attract people to her. She was regarded as a brilliant scientist who should be left alone in order to achieve the maximum.

Recently there were those in the congregation of Tikkun v'Or who suspected her of seeking a loophole to avoid spending a year in Israel. She had social problems even with the most open-minded people in Hebrew Union College, New

York, New York, mainly because of her smoking, but perhaps also because of rumors and envy.

WITH ALL DUE RESPECT to his liberal views, the candidate contending for the presidency seemed to McPhee a really gray character. His skin was gray and he radiated grayness. Perhaps in the end she would vote for the flushed incumbent, who people said was better for Israel.

A black-and-white series from the fifties with Lucille Ball began and Bahat changed channels, while Gruber, in his room, went on watching Archie Bunker. He didn't understand everything; there were some words in English he couldn't get into his head even after their meaning was explained to him a hundred times. "The English is my wife's," he would sometimes say at scientific conferences when beginning the lectures in embarrassing English, which did not embarrass him. The man was so on fire with his own brilliance that he wasn't ashamed of his English.

Bahat wrapped herself in a robe and knocked on his door, she had had it up to here with the volume of these arrogant Israelis who couldn't see anyone else even when they were right under their noses.

Gruber opened the door in his dark blue tracksuit. (When she was alive his wife had classed him as a disappointment, in spite of all his brilliance, and would say to herself, you'll always walk alone, Mandy Greenholtz-Gruber, Mandy G-G, for short.)

"What the fuck are you doing to me!" Bahat upbraided him, "This isn't the corner of Motzkin and Shenkin or whatever you call your streets there. I don't like being woken up at this ungodly hour!"

"Sorry, " muttered the Israeli. "I have *ya-efet*."

"You have what?"

"Jet lag," he made haste to translate the latest innovation of the Hebrew Language Academy.

"Good, and now please keep quiet."

"I'm very sorry," said the guest, "I went too far, I'm very eccentric, my wife says I'm very eccentric too."

"I'm not your wife, but I really need you to be quiet. We have a hard day ahead of us. I have to pass on a ton of secret information to you. I don't feel comfortable about it, I'm afraid that the place is bugged, and that my Hispanic is an FBI plant. Once they even opened a file on Lucille Ball, can you believe it? I have to sleep well and not make any mistakes. I'm an American citizen."

"So what are you saying?" asked Irad, horrified at the possibility that the important information for which he had come all this way would be denied him because of an attack of patriotism.

But she appeared to have returned to her original plans, for she said, "I'm saying that we have to walk a very fine line here and not make a false step in any direction. The key word is balance."

"It's a serious business, I agree," said Irad.

"Then I'll say goodnight," said McPhee and turned to go back to her room. Gruber took a mental photograph of her receding back and the long, thick braid dangling down it. He asked himself if she worked out, and berated himself for not doing so personally.

He tried to go to sleep, but soon gave up and went quietly downstairs. There was a television set on the ground floor too, huge and flat as their own in Telba-North. He muted the sound and switched it on to *All the President's Men*. Luckily he had already seen the movie more than once on cable.

He looked for the light switch in the kitchen and turned on all kinds of lights outside the house, at the bottom of the yard, in the garage, the garbage room, in the garden, apparently to call attention to its beauty, and quickly switched them off again. Judging by this McPhee's sense of proportion, she was liable to accuse him of setting off a fireworks display.

He had never come across a woman with such a short fuse, a fact which he attributed to her genius. There was always a price to pay for genius. In his case, for example, the eccentricity, the egoism, the need for instant gratification. At the cocktail party on the terrace in Jaffa that Mandy had organized after he had received the Israel Prize, he had gotten into conversation with one of the guests, a neurologist if he wasn't mistaken, about the price of genius. The guy, it transpired, had written an article on the subject years ago and had it published in the newspaper *Davar*, now defunct. According to him, the sensitivity of men of genius made it inevitable that their nervous systems would suffer harm. Gruber was embarrassed. Was the man trying to tell him that his nervous system was damaged? "That's the package," said his interlocutor with total confidence, and Gruber beat a hasty retreat before he could present him with the living proof of his thesis.

AT LAST HE FOUND the kitchen light switch and was immediately exposed to a long line of certificates of graduation and distinction hanging on the wall, in botany, zoology, Judaism . . . okay, he had certificates at home too, albeit not hanging on the wall. He looked for her regular coffee and hoped she had regular milk as well, and not that half-and-half.

The coffee machine made a bit of noise and he prayed that Bahat was sound asleep again. In the fridge there was only half-and-half, and Gruber poured the stuff into his coffee, which it turned too white so that he contemplated the result with profound reservations.

He sat down on the sofa opposite the mute television and sipped his coffee. Suddenly he had a good feeling. Maybe because the coffee was good and stimulating. What did he lack? This fullness of being spread through him and he felt, as sometimes happened, that being should be appreciated as such, without all the bullshit of achieving. All in all, what did he have to complain about? He was healthy in body and mind, sitting in the exclusive north of the United States, in the home of an ex-Israeli, drinking coffee, feeling comfortable, even relaxed. Tomorrow, so she said, in other words today, she would pass on to him what she knew about the spider net, and in the meantime until that hour arrived, he would spend the time at his ease. Like now, watching a movie he had already seen and was therefore familiar to him. Those actors were already old. He had seen Dustin Hoffman in a recent movie. But what did Hoffman's age have to do with him?

He stared at the bustling news room of the *Washington Post*, when suddenly on the wall to the right of the television set he noticed a framed official photograph of Richard Nixon himself.

Two puzzling questions occurred to him. Firstly, what did Professor Bahat McPhee have to do with Richard Nixon?

And secondly, wasn't it strange that he should discover this photograph just when they were showing *All the President's Men* on television?

He rose to his feet and went over to the portrait. An old photograph. The president was smiling, so it had apparently been taken before the exposure of the Watergate bugging.

As for the first question he speculated that perhaps he was witness to a pure and simple love of Israel. It was Nixon's airlift during the Yom Kippur War that had saved the state. Did McPhee gain inspiration from the disgraced president and say to herself, if he stood up for Israel why shouldn't I bypass Cornell University, Ithaca City Hall, the Pentagon, and the French health authorities to give the Israelis a bit of a push?

Was she fully aware of the risk she was taking in handing over the vital information about the webs? For a moment he was afraid that the FBI was really watching her and that both of them were going to be thrown into prison for a long time, and made to feel guilty for the massive damage to the relations between Israel and the United States.

Who would be crazy enough to take the risk of damaging Israel's relations with the USA, especially after Nixon's airlift?

Gruber broke out in a sweat. Not only had he not thought his plans through to the end, he hadn't thought *at all* when he applied for approval for his flight to the US after the occurrence of Titanic three.

He decided that if they were caught he would pin all the blame on her, he would say that the subterfuge was all on her initiative, while he himself believed that the financial backers and the Americans were in on the collaboration. He didn't have the least idea that she was acting behind the back of the Pentagon, which in his opinion was unforgivable in such sensitive times.

He was deterred by the situation in which he found himself, and all he wanted was to be back in Israel with the information he needed and to forget everything that had gone before. Shimon Peres himself had told him personally, at some dinner, that spies took the risk of being forgotten in jail, and even worse, every novice spy knew that he had to be prepared for the total denial of the state in the event of his being caught. Peres had stressed that it was the most treacherous profession in the world. And indeed, what if the state were to deny out of hand that he had come to America at its behest and then accuse him of coming here on his own private business, for his personal profit? They might even say that he planned to convert his wife's pajama factory, Nighty-Night, and manufacture T-suits for export to China!

A deep sense of uneasiness in the face of something a lot bigger than he was took hold of him. The coffee was tasteless, and in any case he had already finished it. His mood changed completely. He felt really uncomfortable. What if they put him in a cell with someone from al-Qaeda?

A taxi stopped outside McPhee's house and let off a passenger. This was already too much for the Israeli scientist. He was convinced that an FBI agent had arrived, or an officer from some secret police force, which had been set up to deal with all kinds of eventualities after 9/11 and received an additional impetus after the bombings in Madrid and London. He reminded himself to deny everything out of hand. He would say that he had no idea McPhee was working behind the back of American interests, on the contrary! But at the thought of the diplomatic imbroglio, perhaps even the political earthquake to come, the scientist succumbed to an acute attack of vertigo.

Due to the vertigo, and also to the terror he felt both before and during the vertigo, in other words the terror of the vertigo itself, Gruber failed to notice that the man at the door had a large white parrot on his shoulder, something which immediately negated the possibility of his being an agent of the FBI. He also failed to notice the fact that the man had a distinctly Israeli appearance and a medium-sized suitcase on wheels.

The man rang the doorbell and Gruber went to open it. How great was his surprise when the man opened the door himself, with his own key.

Now the two of them stood facing each other, and Gruber didn't know what language to speak.

The uninvited guest was not surprised to see Gruber, and said in Hebrew:

"Shalom, are you Dr. Gruber from Israel?"

Gruber nodded.

"I'm Professor Raffi Propheta, Berkeley University Hebrew studies, how do you do? Allow me to add that I am also a good friend and well-wisher of Bahat McPhee."

6

THE TIME WAS 4:30 A.M. ACCORDING TO THE KITCHEN clock. No mentality, even the Levantine, approved of ringing somebody's doorbell at this hour unless something had happened. Professor Propheta opened and shut kitchen cupboards as if the place belonged to him, all with the parrot on his shoulder. Gruber watched him.

"You want chai?" he asked Gruber.

"No, thank you," he said, "I already had coffee."

"You want another cup?"

"No, thank you."

He looked like a bitter and perhaps aggressive man, but not dangerous. His bearing was stooped, almost feeble, and the contribution of his spine to his posture wasn't clear.

"Don't you drink chai over there in Israel?" he asked.

"My wife does," said Gruber and began to smell the aroma of the ginger, familiar from home.

"Your wife is very wise," said Propheta.

He didn't like the look of this Propheta. He didn't look good for his age, or not for his age either.

He was half bald, short, running to fat of the flabby kind. And on his bearded face, with the dusty looking mustache, was a sulky expression. He filled Gruber with a sense of defeat.

In order to recover, Gruber could have scolded him for his intrusion at this ungodly hour, and thus externalized his aversion to the man, but there was something pitiful about Propheta, and Gruber really did feel pity for him, especially when he saw that his hands trembled slightly—before, when he was peeling the ginger, and also now, as he poured the milk into the chai.

When he turned to face Gruber, with the hot drink in his hand and the parrot that didn't budge from his shoulder, he complained that he couldn't find the cardamom among Bahat's spices, either she didn't have any or she had run out, and Gruber noticed that the anger on his face was out of proportion to the offense, that the man presumably wore a permanent expression of anger and accusation. Although he had thought at first that the intruder was simply worn out after the journey from Berkeley to San Francisco, and from San Francisco to New York, and from New York to Ithaca, he now realized that the Hebrew teacher from Berkeley was a man full of rage.

AND HE HAD SOMETHING to be enraged about! As an aperitif, Propheta was angry about having to leave his post at the University of Montpelier in the south of France and move to the USA, and to the ends of the earth what's more, to Berkeley.

The USA and France seemed to Propheta like two different planets, and he was unable to make the transition smoothly, so that part of him always remained in Israel, another part in Montpelier, and now he had to manage with what was left.

For three years now he had been outside Western Europe, and he yearned to go back there, but he didn't have a hope.

All the senior positions in Western Europe were taken, and he refused to go to Eastern Europe or to Scandinavia, even though he had offers. In Europe it was easier to forget the pains of life, he thought. In Europe you weren't alone. There were other people, and you could talk to them. They answered you. In the USA people were always asking you how you were, and if you answered them seriously, you found yourself talking to thin air, as had happened to him more than once. The question "How are you?" wasn't a question at all, it was just a greeting.

Every day outside of Europe was a waste of time, especially in view of the fact that Hebrew studies in Berkeley were at an all-time low since the outbreak of the second Intifada, and he, like other Hebrew professors in the USA, had to be grateful that their departments hadn't been shut down due to a lack of interest, as had already happened in a few places, like Yale, for example.

It may well be that it was this lack of interest on the part of the Americans in Hebrew culture that had prompted Propheta himself to stop taking an interest in Hebrew literature. Although he went on teaching as usual, sometimes even he felt like walking out of his own classes.

And this being the case, a great void opened up in Propheta's life. And he filled this void with geopolitics, a field in which he began to be very interested, and also, in his opinion, to master.

He was of the opinion that the period of the beginning of the third millennium, in other words right now, was of unparalleled importance, and that the future of humanity would be determined by the people who set the tone. Propheta wanted to set the tone, but first he set out to master the contents. And in the meantime, so as not to cut himself off from the revolution, in a special notebook he wrote down all the great events all over the world, including in Chechnya, and also in all kinds of African states that didn't even have a functioning state. He wrote down everything in a clear hand in a special notebook, in case there wouldn't be any computers after the world was destroyed.

Recently Propheta had published a book of his own on the subject of contemporary politics, intended to sell for eleven dollars to students of international relations so that if they didn't have a clue about what was happening, his words would reverberate inside them. To the students of Hebrew at Berkeley, fifteen in all, he distributed the book for free.

The First Autoimmune Period—this was the title of his book, and its thesis was that the new terror should be fought in the same way as autoimmune diseases. "What is happening here?" he asked in his book. "The world should be seen as a human body that fails to perceive something as friendly, and attacks it. Wake up sick world! Build alternatives!" he cried, without going into details.

His book was relatively thin, one hundred and forty pages in all, and it ended with a call to action. Professor Propheta called on psychologists and depth psychologists to found a new psychology that would explain what *was* happening and what *had* happened in the soul of the contemporary terrorist to make him want to carry out a large scale, disturbing act of destruction.

The confused citizens of the world had the right to receive a more serious explanation than "these people are insane."

The terrorists who emerged from the refugee camps or from the heart of one or another European capital were not crazy people. Their acts had a rational explanation, and it had to be discovered. Reading between the lines it was evident that he was unimpressed by chaos theory, and that he scorned those who relied on it to provide a so-called explanation, while in fact they were throwing sand in the eyes of the confused citizens seeking peace and justice.

Psychologists were falling down on the job, they had to set everything else aside and concentrate on the question of how to identify potential terrorists in childhood, and to prevent them, through educational means, from reaching such extremes. He did not rule out the possibility that early signs of the potential for destruction might even be identified in future terrorists while still in the mother's womb.

Until white smoke rises! he demanded. They had to work on it until the personality structure of the suicide bomber was exposed! For example, to understand why he didn't put an end to his life on his own, alone in his room, or in a solitary spot in the bosom of nature, why he insisted on taking other people with him. And the brilliant minds should also identify the personality structures of those who *sent* the suicide bombers. What kind of psychological projection led a man to send someone else to commit suicide, instead of committing suicide himself? And this information should be made available to everybody. He demanded transparency!

His book was full of exclamation marks, which made his readers feel uneasy.

He was interviewed in the local Berkeley paper, and he explained his positions in detail, but the interview only received one short, thin column, accompanying a terrible passport photo (the one from his green card), and it read that a new book had been published by an ex-Israeli who argued that many Israelis, in contrast to himself, had lost their minds because of the occupation, and that he, whose mind was clear and lucid, wanted to warn people that the world was about to be destroyed, with Israel at the top of the list.

Propheta was insulted at having been mentioned in the context of the occupation when he had sought to write an abstract book, and tried to make sure that the word "occupation" didn't appear in it even once.

In the last chapter of the book he asserted unequivocally that the human race had embarked on its suicidal autoimmune journey with two important historical events: the rise of Khomeinism, and the fall of the walls between East and West, which had completely confused the world. He hinted that the fall of the walls had been a calamity for mankind.

But he also had a consoling, optimistic message. In the end, humanity would be saved thanks to the Chinese. The Chinese, who constituted a very serious slice of the global population, would realize that there was no other nation capable of overcoming the dangerous autoimmunism that had invaded the human race. And then, with Confucian discipline and an emphasis on bureaucracy and minute detail, the Chinese would take over the world, which by then would be almost completely virtual, and set it to order, in their Chinese way.

ALL THIS, more or less, Propheta told Gruber while standing up and sipping his chai, with the smell of the ginger spreading through Bahat's living room. In the end it didn't make a big impression on Gruber, in spite of the dramatic silence with which Propheta concluded his words. The parrot too, which had flown off his shoulder and was standing on the table, seemed indifferent.

"Where did you meet Bahat McPhee?" asked Gruber.

"The first time was on the forum on Rod Serling, if you're familiar with the name. But the second time I met her was at the JCC, the Jewish Community Center in Berkeley, on the ninth anniversary of Rabin's assassination. There was some Israeli klutz there who talked about economics and corporations, as if it had anything to do with Rabin's murder, and I shouted 'Murderer, murderer!' from the audience, and she tried to calm me down, but I was already in a trance. 'You killed fifteen Arab kids then, you're criminals, but that's a different matter.'"

"But why blame the lecturer for corporations?"

"He's morally responsible. Anyone who doesn't leave Israel, like I did by the way, bears moral responsibility. After a few years of seeing the damage done to the Israelis by the occupation, I picked up my heels and made for France. It was only there that I began to live. And when I say 'live', I don't mean 'survive.'"

"Obviously," said Gruber.

"They removed me from the hall and Bahat came with me, even though she doesn't hold my opinions. From then we've been friends, in spite of the ideological chasm. She says that the law of sympathy according to Gershom Scholem operates between us."

"I never read him," said Gruber.

"Neither did I. But it's something in the kabbalah. About souls knowing each other from previous incarnations, and the law of sympathy operates between them. She says that kind of sympathy exists between us, mystical."

"You know what?" said Gruber, "I will have chai."

"Really?" Propheta said, pleased. "I'm the chai champion of Berkeley."

"I'm sure you are."

7

"WHERE IS SHE?" ASKED PROPHETA, STEPPING CAREFULLY with two fresh cups of chai toward Gruber, who was sitting in front of the television and watching the end of *All the President's Men*. Again the smell of the ginger pervaded the living room. Propheta took a coaster from a little stack of rubber coasters standing on the table, and Gruber followed his movements with interest. He couldn't remember if they had this same custom at home, or if Mandy served tea and coffee in cups with saucers, making coasters unnecessary.

The arguments between Mandy and Lirit on this subject had been completely wiped out of his memory. Lirit would drink hot drinks from a mug without using a coaster. If there was one thing Mandy couldn't stand, it was rings on tables. In other people's houses too, she would wonder how they could leave rings on tables that had cost thousands of dollars. It seemed crude and Israeli to her.

"Where is she?" Propheta asked again after blowing on his cup.

"Sleeping," said Gruber.

"You don't know how happy I am now," Propheta said suddenly, as if this time there was something special in the chai, "You know, just talking Hebrew. Not that I have a problem with English. I speak English like an American, I pick up languages quickly. It goes without saying that if I taught Hebrew in Montpellier, French isn't a problem for me either, but when I speak Hebrew," his eyes shot sparks of happiness, "I can give my facial muscles a rest. And relaxing the facial muscles relaxes areas in my brain. And I won't say it isn't a pleasure. And this is after living outside Israel for years."

He sat down on the sofa next to Gruber, not in order to watch the end of the movie, but in order to speak Hebrew.

Gruber pretended to be radically interested in the movie. He narrowed his eyes in order to catch every word, even though it wasn't up to the eyes to hear, and Propheta understood his body language and kept quiet.

"What do you think of her house?" he asked after a while.

"I don't know what to tell you," said Gruber, who, because he was so surprised by the question, answered it honestly, "On the one hand it's young girl's apartment, and on the other hand an old woman's, with all this pseudo-antique kitsch. There's no direction. Did you see the photograph of Richard Nixon? What's the nature of her relationship with the Hispanic bio-technologist?"

"I think pure sex, and that it's over. Ever since the business of Reform Judaism came into the picture, she put a stop to it, because he's uncircumcised."

Gruber paid no attention to his words and continued:

"My wife wouldn't have looked at this place even if it was on the seashore. My wife really likes living next to the sea. When she was a child she lived in Tel Aviv not far from the sea, and ever since then the sea is an essential view-supplement for her."

"Do you live next to the sea?" asked Propheta, listening with half an ear.

"No. We live in Tel Baruch North. Do you know it?"

"I'm from Motza, next to Jerusalem."

"Tell me, do you think I don't know that Motza is next to Jerusalem?"

"Until the age of fifteen," added Propheta. "After that we moved to Beit Zayit. My parents are still there. In a retirement village, but every day at five in the morning they go to the pool."

Gruber didn't ask him if he missed the views of the Jerusalem hills because he wasn't interested, and in any case, Bahat McPhee was coming down the stairs in neurotic overload. She needed her pills. By the way she walked Propheta could tell that she was suffering from some chemical deprivation or other and that there was no point in talking to her until the chemistry kicked in.

Gruber, ignorant of the problem, stood up.

"Hi, good morning to you."

She didn't answer. She walked past them on her way to the kitchen, returned with a bottle of Coca-Cola she had taken out of the fridge, and swallowed the pills clenched in her fist with the help of a sip straight from the bottle.

Gruber said, "In our family everyone has his own drink. My wife introduced this rule so that no one would drink from anyone else's bottle, on grounds of hygiene."

"Do you want to drink cola from a bottle?" asked Bahat quietly. "I have a stock of bottles. But not cold."

"I never drink straight from the bottle," said Gruber, untruthfully.

Propheta felt a little pang of jealousy, but which he knew was not legitimate. Although he realized that Bahat was not yet focused, he was insulted by the fact that she had not responded to his presence. He hadn't expected her to fall into his arms, but nor had he expected her to ignore him.

McPhee wondered if she had given him some kind of hint to come. And even if she had, it was a mistake, and she wanted to get rid of him.

But Propheta was determined to protect Bahat McPhee and had no intention of leaving her alone with any devious Israelis. If she didn't realize that she was being exploited, then thank God he was here. The woman was about to give away to Israel information she had worked on for years, often at the expense of her social life. He thought that if she was really going to give them the right answers, then she had to demand money in return. And there was no reason for her to tell the rabbi from Albany about it. Not everyone had to know everything about everybody.

But he knew that McPhee was set on feeling noble, and that if she took even a single dollar from the Israeli she would feel as if she had betrayed herself.

Bahat, in the end, was a very lonely woman. People who used to be her friends and who used to call her occasionally had deserted her out of consideration because they had persuaded themselves that they didn't want to disturb the genius at her research. Because of everything she had gone through in her life, and because of her years of loneliness, she tended to lose her sense of proportion and she needed someone to supervise her judgment. Which is where he, Propheta, came into the picture.

He held the opinion that she had been through enough, by which he meant the affair with Emily Boston, and the whole mess that came after it when Randall left her his parents to take care of until the day they died.

He wasn't going to let anyone hurt this woman, whom he regarded as an angel in human form.

The truth was that Propheta was in love with her, but he knew that she couldn't stand him physically. To him Bahat was a breath of fresh air in his world, and her social isolation touched his heart. She was mistaken in thinking that when she was a Reform rabbi she would meet people in the framework of her routine, and that they would have to be nice to her, that she would make friends with some of them, and then perhaps she would also find some lover she could stand physically and in whom she would find all the qualities her heart desired, at least for a few years because she was already sick to death of being with spiders all day long.

Propheta was also suspicious of the rabbi from Albany, but he had no way of approaching her. What kind of a person was she? How could the rabbi allow this woman—who anyone could see had been disappointed by the world and who was acting out of utter despair—to pour years of her hard work into the hands of the Israelis? If he understood correctly, she was actually giving up her chance for a Nobel here, and perhaps even risking her liberty. Harming the security of the United States was the last thing she needed.

On the other hand, the danger to relations between the USA and the State of Israel didn't interest him so much as a hair of his mustache, which had once been ginger and was now a yellowish gray. On this point Propheta thought that as a logistics officer in the reserves he was no mean strategist because he was perhaps the only one here who thought things through to the end.

BAHAT SAW THE TRANSMISSION of information to Gruber as an excellent way out of the condition of being buried alive that she had organized for herself over the past few years. When she set the two things opposite each other—the modification of the gene responsible for the activity of the spinning glands in the spiders, opposite the title of Reform rabbi, which meant a lively social life, and what's more, one without feeling that she was imposing herself on people because she would be serving them by the very fact of her presence—it was very clear to her which of the two she preferred.

The sign that she was doing the right thing she found in the terrible headaches which assailed her before she had decided between the two. As long as they continued, alternating between the left side of her head and then the right, she felt torn between her loyalty to the United States and her loyalty to herself. But the moment she made up her mind, they vanished into thin air.

"I don't feel like coffee," she suddenly said sadly, and it seemed that only then she noticed the presence of the parrot that was now perched on the windowsill. But she ignored it.

"Do you want me to make you chai?" asked Propheta happily.

"Yes, but I haven't got any cardamom."

"I know you haven't. I took note of it," he smiled at her and she smiled back at him, a perfunctory smile, not from the heart but out of embarrassment.

McPhee approached the sofa where Gruber was sitting.

"After the chai we'll go to visit my spider farm," she said. "And in the meantime the pills will take effect."

"What pills do you take?" asked Gruber with affected empathy.

"None of your business," she said, and he was horrified by her bluntness.

Suddenly breaking news came on the television. A mass terror attack in Geneva. The first pictures. Exclusive.

All three turned their eyes to the screen, two of them as if what was now being shown on the television was an earthquake of seven points on the Richter scale in the third world. There were things that had to be done.

"Is anywhere safe from them?" murmured Gruber in the voice of decent humanity.

Propheta said, "It would be better if I didn't say what I think."

"Much better," said Bahat carelessly.

Propheta was insulted again, but what could he do. This was the path he had chosen.

"I have to phone home. I haven't spoken to my family since I arrived," said Gruber urgently, as if the attack had taken place in Israel and his family was in danger.

"It must be night in Israel," said Propheta without a second thought.

"Ahh," said Gruber, "my wife must be sleeping. She goes to bed at nine o'clock. My son, if he isn't sleeping, is taking part in some targeted intervention. And my daughter is singing lullabies to her boyfriend's organic vegetables in the Negev. I'll call them in a few hours' time. So they won't be worried about me."

8

IN THE MORNING, AFTER EVERYONE HAD GONE TO WORK, Lirit sat in the shopping center Mikado in Café au Lait, where they only served coffee without milk in special circumstances, and she waited for ages for the latte in a mug she had ordered. Lirit really wanted to complain to the owner, but what good would it do her. She surveyed the scene. In a shallow pool eight disciplined openings gave rise to a meter-and-a-half high jet, which fell dead straight onto itself, God forbid a drop should stray from the regime imposed on it by the designer. They told the designer without a lot of splashing, and he did as he was told. To the left was a pizza parlor called Big Apple Pizza. The shopping center was quite empty, because the children who usually hung out there were in school. At last they had opened a school here in the neighborhood. The mothers had been going crazy from driving their kids to distant schools every morning.

The latte in a mug arrived and Lirit told the waitress that she had been waiting for more than ten minutes. The waitress replied that that was how long you waited here for latte in a mug.

Lirit didn't like coffee. But a day and a bit after her mother's death, this was the least she could do in her memory: drink a latte in a mug. She didn't yet feel pain at the loss. She was indifferent, as if nothing had happened. Perhaps it was the shock, she thought to herself.

Earlier that morning she had quarreled with Dael, who wanted to return to his base. He said that in any case there was no funeral because their mother had donated her body to science, and no shivah either, and in any case they had lost track of their father in the USA, and they didn't want to see anybody anyway—so what the point in him staying?

In the end Lirit thought that he was right, and he went back to the field. But yesterday he had managed to take care of placing death notices in the street and in the three newspapers. On the way to the café Lirit passed one of the notices and read it. Lirit thought generally that perhaps she would study graphic design. She had never actually read a death notice before. And one about her mother too.

She looked round and came across more death notices about her mother, as well as one about somebody else whose family had gone for a normal funeral in Kiryat Shaul. What was all this bereavement suddenly? She was angry because it seemed so irrelevant to her family. They whole place suddenly seemed to her like some habitation of ghosts. She had hardly made it to Café au Lait.

It jarred her to see her mother's name plastered all over Alexander Penn Street, but that was the reality, she reminded herself again. Twice she stopped to read the notices that Dael had composed for the street. The other one he published in the newspapers. While she drank her coffee she went over both of them in her mind:

Our beloved
Amanda (Mandy) Gruber née Greenholtz

Has suddenly left us
And donated her body to science.
Please refrain from condolence calls.
Her dear ones.

And the notice in the newspapers said:

The textile factory Nighty-Night
Bows its head
At the untimely death of its manager
Amanda (Mandy) Gruber of blessed memory,
A warm, diligent, and benevolent woman,
And offers its condolences to the family.

After she finished her coffee she had no idea what to do with herself. She was simply completely paralyzed, but it was clear to her, and this actually helped her, that she wasn't going to any factory today. At maximum, she would answer the phone in the event that people from the factory, or her father's jet set, wanted to offer their condolences. But people would want to know how, when, why she died, and Lirit didn't have the motivation to tell the whole story of her deterioration over and over again. She decided that never mind the gossip and the rumors, she was going to disconnect all the telephones.

But what if her father called? How could she disconnect the phones? But screen the calls, yes. Local calls she could screen, but if there was an unidentified caller, and it turned out not to be her father, she would just say it was the wrong number.

She went back to staring at the fountain with the jet falling onto itself, and she remembered how her mother used to say that it wouldn't do anybody in the Levant any good, however much they played at being in Europe or Los Angeles, they didn't have the first idea about aesthetics. "It's only now that they're beginning to get it into their heads, Liritush," she said to her once, "but they're already in the swing of building a state and they can't change their style."

She couldn't remember if her mother had made any criticisms of Tel Baruch North as well. Lirit actually thought that the fact that there wasn't a drop of Zionism in the place made it international, and the fact that there wasn't any socialism made it progressive. True, she didn't say this out loud, because of Shlomi, who after his one-time visit said that it was enough to look at the people's faces and see how they behaved to conclude that they were hedonistic Israelis in a new suburb of North Tel Aviv, interested in nothing but themselves.

And indeed, after sitting there staring for an hour she could see so for herself: women a little bit older than she was, and also of thirty and forty plus, all of them with Ray-Ban glasses, smartly dressed from top to toe, going from shop to shop, and parallel to them, grannies with pigmentation problems running after grandchildren, one or two of whom were escaping in the direction of the escalators and standing there wailing at the top of their voices, and in the end the grannies gave in and rode up and down the moving stairs again and again and again. Where was she going to get the patience for all this?

No pause in the routine in memory of the dead Mandy. Everything as usual. Lirit looked at a new clothing store that called itself FREEDOM. Opposite it in a Delta store, there was an end of the season sale of tank tops for toddlers: three for sixteen dollars. She thought that everything here was relatively cute, but she didn't have the strength for it now. The coffee had not woken her up, it had made her want to go to sleep, or more precisely, to disappear.

She was only twenty-two, and her mother's death was really too heavy for her. And she hadn't really taken in the fact yet that she had inherited a pajama factory that marketed its products to the ultra-orthodox sector, and that she had to pick up the pieces and step smartly into her mother's shoes.

BUT TOWARD NOON she called Nighty-Night on her cell phone, and told her mother's right-hand woman, Carmela Levy, that she wouldn't be coming in for the next few days. But of course she wouldn't be coming in, said Carmela Levy, and Lirit, who was still sitting in Cafe au Lait listened to a few more condolences, including wonder at the fact that the deceased had donated her body to science and had not asked for a civil burial in a coffin, which would have been far more her style, like the soldiers in the IDF. The two of them had talked about it. But now perhaps she too would donate her body to science.

Suddenly Lirit understood that science benefited from the dead who donated their bodies to it, and that science was actually humanity, and that it was a kind of feedback. She herself didn't want to be part of this feedback, with all due respect to the cycles in nature. In order to get away from the subject of bodies and science, Lirit said in a gloomy voice that ever since the blow that had come down on them, she couldn't leave the house, and she even wondered if she should tell Carmela that they had lost contact with their father. But in the end it was lucky that she didn't tell her, or she would have kept her for another half an hour on the phone.

In conclusion Lirit asked her to convey a message to the workers. She knew—she stressed in a tone that sounded a bit as if she was on television—that her mother would have asked them to carry on. Despite everything. To sew. To work. To produce. Not to let her death confuse them and weaken their resolve. That is what she would have wanted.

"Definitely," said Carmela in an almost holy tone.

AFTER THE CONVERSATION Carmela retired to some corner in the factory yard behind a tree, and cried, and wiped her eyes with the cloth handkerchief she kept about her person, as her boss had done, God bless her soul. She had learned many delicacies and refinements from her.

She was also anxious about the future. Judging by what she had heard from Mandy over the years, she had good reason to fear Lirit. Lirit was unpredictable. It was Carmela who had given Mandy the advice worth its weight in gold to give Lucas money and send him back to Jamaica. Lately, with Lirit living with someone twice her age, Carmela Levy had waited together with Mandy Gruber for the affair to come to a sticky end.

ONLY ON HER WAY HOME did Lirit realize that she had no more economic problems. It was a reassuring thought, and she made up her mind not to change anything in the short term, to study the subject even though she already knew it, having spent whole summers helping her mother manage the business.

She thought about the long term when she got home, and

considered her sudden freedom. What was she going to do in the long term? She didn't know. Perhaps she would turn Nighty-Night inside out, perhaps she would at long last renovate the place outside and especially inside, and march it into the twenty-first century.

It wasn't at all impossible that she would examine, in the long term of course, the necessity of at long last changing the target market for the pajamas, and also of touching on the holy of holies, the five patterns exclusive to Nighty-Night, which had long been out of date. Mandy was as stubborn as a mule: she was prepared for there to be only stripes, in two versions; checks, in a one-and-only version for all ages; one floral pattern; and also a pajama in a plain fabric, but in all colors.

The patterns had hardly changed at all since Audrey's time and to the new heir they seemed old fashioned and even repulsive, but in the meantime her mother's ghost prevented her from coming to any decision.

She sat down on the sofa and sank into a black mood.

Is this it? she asked herself. Am I going to be buried in a pajama factory for the ultra-Orthodox from now on? Forever? Is this my life? Is this my vocation? Warp and woof for cold nights with no fear of impurities?

She sighed and tried to comfort herself that it wasn't the end of the world even though it was the end of the world for her, and that perhaps she should take a bold step and transfer production to Turkey or China, and in Israel she would get someone else to do the marketing and who would work on commission. In the space of five minutes Lirit made a hundred decisions, including selling the factory, running away and leaving everything to Dael and their father, marrying

Shlomi and then getting divorced from him. Somewhere or other in the framework of what might be called Lirit's Dream, there was also a plan for an exclusive line of organic cotton (that would be without any fear whatsoever of impurities), which went hand in hand with the overall renovation of the factory.

THE PHONE RANG. On the screen of her upgraded cell phone she saw that it was an overseas call. Instead of rushing to reply, she let it ring, and only after seven or eight rings she took a deep breath and answered. A hard task awaited her.

But her father never let the flow of his words arrest itself, and as usual she couldn't get a word in edgeways. Right off he started talking in a big hurry, as if he was speaking on a pay phone and he had no more change left. All the urgency in the world belonged to him. It was inconceivable that something fateful could have happened somewhere else.

He was sorry for not being in contact for the past three days, but he had forgotten his cell phone in Israel, and also he needed the holiday, especially as it wasn't a holiday at all, it was work. There wasn't a lot left, they had already been working for four days. He was taking what he required for the continuation of his TESU research and coming home in a day or two. It was morning where he was now, and what was the time over there? He was very happy and satisfied and eager to get back with the results.

He sounded distant and strange to her. She couldn't believe that he was the only parent they had left, Dael and she. Would it occur to him to ask how she was? How his wife was? Usually he called to hear himself talking to his family.

Lirit let him finish his monologue down to the last detail, including the fact that he was now in the laboratory with his American colleague, and only then, a second before he was about to say goodbye, she delivered the bitter blow in full.

"Why are you only telling me now?" her father yelled down the line, "What are you saying to me all of a sudden?"

At this point there was silence, as if they had been disconnected, and Lirit asked twice, "Hello?" and then,

"Daddy, are you all right?"

"I'm here, I'm here," he said weakly, and suddenly he seemed to wake up, "What do you mean she donated her body to science? Is she crazy?"

"So there's no funeral, right? Only after six months or something?" he added after another silence.

"Yes," said Lirit.

"I don't understand this business of donating to science," he said, "It isn't her style."

"That's what she wanted," said Lirit.

Only now he asked how she was bearing up, and without waiting for an answer he asked how Dael was.

She said that she hadn't taken it in yet. It all seemed like a dream. Everything was falling apart. And how was she going to take her mother's place at the factory, because that was what Mandy wanted? And altogether, how was she going to go on living without her? And without Shlomi too, because they'd split up. And how were they going to get through this hell by themselves, with him far away?

In the face of so many questions, her father asked her first of all to calm down. After that he gathered his strength and told her that however hard it was—and he knew that it was terrible for her, really devastating, and he too felt very bad about it—she should please, please introduce a little logic into the situation.

"I'm trying, I'm trying," said Lirit.

In fact, it was clear to her that this would be the first or second thing that he would say, that she should introduce logic into the situation. Anyone whose life went off the rails, and who saw it fit to confide in her father, was told to please introduce logic into the situation.

"Good," said her father, and added, "Be strong, Liritush. Be strong."

And then,

"Listen, Liritush, I'm a little stunned and confused, darling, I'll call again later."

ACROSS THE OCEAN Bahat looked at Irad with great compassion, but also with concern. She didn't understand much from what she could gather from the telephone conversation. Only that someone, perhaps a close friend of his daughter's, had died and had donated her body to science, and that his daughter was in a state of total collapse. Would he shorten his stay here in order to be with her? He refused to answer her repeated question, what happened, and returned immediately to the computer. But his silence was suspicious. Was she witnessing a new chaos breaking into her life? Were all her plans about to blow up in her face? It had taken her two days before she succeeded in tactfully getting rid of Propheta, that Jew who was sick with some mental disease that didn't interest her. He had appointed himself her bodyguard and prevented them from getting on with their work. Only yesterday and today were they finally making progress.

She looked at Gruber, who went on browsing in the

depths of the computer as if nothing had happened, but who looked as if he was going to faint.

"I've had a terrible shock," he said suddenly. "I feel giddy. My pulse must be racing. Maybe I'm going to faint. Maybe I'm starting a heart attack."

"Maybe you'll tell me at last what exactly happened?" asked Bahat and came closer.

"My wife died from plastic surgery," he said.

"So that's it! How terrible! Would you like a glass of water?"

"Please," mumbled Gruber and held his heart.

She went to fetch him a glass of water.

"There's no need to sink into the deep mire," she said from a distance, "It's a terrible shock, but there's no need to descend into a low dungeon. You'll go home and attend to things. At times like this you should be strong and practical. Do you understand me? *You* need to introduce logic into the situation. *You* need to be strong in order to take care of your children, who must be in a bad way. You said that she donated her body to science? So there's no reason to get pressured about the funeral . . ."

Gruber had already fainted on the floor. Bahat was in a panic. Leah Shlezinger, the Reform rabbi from Albany, was supposed to come the next day to get Gruber's signature on the secret document that would enable Bahat to obtain her title in exchange for transmitting information to Israel. The two of them were supposed to confirm to the rabbi that Bahat hadn't received any kickbacks and that she had performed an act of pure charity for the sake of the State of Israel.

One sentence had stayed with her from the book which had helped her to prepare for her matriculation exam in

Jewish history: "Ze'ev Tiomkin's plans burst like a bubble of suds." She refused to let her plans burst like a bubble of suds.

"You mustn't break," she murmured. "You have to go on. Wake up, Dr. Gruber, wake up." She shook him, slapped him, poured water on him, and cried, "Please, Dr. Gruber, don't despair. We can't let them break us. Please."

He opened his eyes.

"Did I faint?" he asked.

"Yes." Bahat went on dripping water onto his face and spreading it over his forehead and cheeks.

"Breathe slowly, everything's going to be all right."

"Did you call an ambulance?" he asked.

"No, no, there's no need to call an ambulance for everything. Look, you're awake. You're alive. Be grateful. Sometimes you can pull through on your own, without drama! This isn't a play. We're only human . . ."

Gruber didn't listen to her. He was in shock.

"I have to go back!" he said.

"Of course you do, there's no question about it. But in the meantime, before you go back, I'll bring you another glass of water."

She hurried to bring him cold water. He drank.

"Look," she said to him, "in any case she donated her body to science, so there's no need for you to hurry back, you can complete your mission."

"What an idiot . . ." mumbled Gruber.

"Who?" asked Bahat apprehensively.

"My wife. An idiot plain and simple. All those plastic surgeries, it all came back to her like a boomerang. It's hard to believe that I'm a *widower*. The title doesn't suit me at all. I'm the most vital man in the world."

9

LIRIT LIT A CIGARETTE. AT LAST SHE HAD HANDED OVER the management of the crisis to her father. She sat on the sofa and waited for a lightening of the load, but to her surprise she failed to feel it. She regretted not having taken that American woman's phone number from her father. She reached out for the *Haaretz* newspaper and put it on her lap with the intention of leafing through it, but her eyes were full of tears. For the first time since her mother's death, she wept. She put the paper down and shook her head from side to side as if to say she didn't believe it, she refused to accept it.

The Grubers subscribed to *Haaretz*, *L'Isha*, French *Vogue*, *Marie Claire* in English, and the American *Cosmopolitan*. In addition their mailbox was always full of scientific journals in various fields for her father, and professional journals in the textile field for her mother.

Lirit saw that she was out of cigarettes, and she took Mandy's handbag and set out for the shopping center to replenish her supply. As she crossed the road on her way to Mikado, she was assailed by the smell of sewage. She looked around her and she couldn't understand where it was coming from. After all, the neighborhood was a new one and you weren't supposed to smell the drains.

Now she noticed the foreign workers busy at the manholes, shouting instructions to each other in perfect Hebrew. She understood that they were foreign only when she heard the Israeli driver of the sewage truck talking to them.

Lirit spoke to the owner of the snack shop about the smell.

"It's a horrible smell, I know," he said. "It puts my customers off. Takes away their appetite for cracking sunflower seeds. But the ones who suffer most are the clothing stores. Nobody wants to choose clothes under the pressure of a stinky smell."

"What happened?" asked Lirit as he counted her change.

"There's some foul up in the main pipelines of the neighborhood. I don't know if you've had a whiff of what's going on in the underground parking garage."

"No," said Lirit. "I live opposite."

The man from the snack shop said: "I'm telling you, I only park my car outside, because on minus two, and sometimes even on minus one, you can die from the smell. My boss told me to say that it's temporary, so that's what I'm telling you: it's temporary. They're taking care of it."

Lirit pulled a smiling face, which she had learned and copied from her mother, and turned round to go home. Many things caught her eye, there was no doubt that her point of view had changed completely and she was now like a butterfly in a field of spring flowers. If her prehistoric Shlomi was right and it was impossible to swim in the same river twice, and the main thing in life was change itself—Shlomi said that change contained a lot of fire energy—then why shouldn't she embark on a shopping expedition now in this Mikado, with her mother's credit card, as long as it hadn't been cancelled? What was stopping her? Who would stop her?

She scolded herself that it wasn't nice, but nevertheless,

in spite of the smell, she went into the opticians and tried on a pair of sunglasses for two hundred dollars that looked great on her, and paid with her mother's credit card, but on the slip she signed Gruber without forging her mother's signature. There were limits.

Afterward she went on looking the place over. She went into Nine One One and bought three tight-fitting tops, which in the past, with Shlomi, she wouldn't have dared to wear because of their price.

She went home to rest, and made up her mind that after taking a little nap, because she was feeling giddy from the terrible smell, she would call a taxi (why waste time looking for parking in Tel Aviv?) and go to Dizengoff Center to continue what she had only just begun. If her father called her on her cell phone, first, she didn't have to answer, and second, she didn't owe him an account of her whereabouts, in a fitting room for example.

She would get the details of his return flight, and tell him that she would come and pick him up at the airport. He was her father, after all.

SHE STAYED IN THE CENTER for about five hours. She progressed at her leisure, going from shop to shop. At last she could buy clothes she hadn't even dared to want to buy when she was attached to Shlomi and under her mother's moral supervision. She remembered how at the beginning of their relationship he already had the nerve to insist that she get rid of her previous wardrobe, which included things worth thousands of dollars, like original designer outfits from Paris, Rome, and London. Because of these outfits her mother hadn't spoken to her for three days from the minute the credit card charge showed up, but in the end she was forced to admit that Lirit looked fantastic in them. All her clothes, including the stunning shoes she had bought in Manhattan when she traveled to that island after the army, everything, in his presence she had thrown into the collection bin for the poverty stricken of the settler town of Netivot. Shlomi photographed the event, symbolic to him and meaningful to her, with his Minolta camera. They were very much in love, and Lirit was smiling in the photographs.

Now she wanted to renew herself and forget the past. She was obviously suffering mental distress. Not being a particularly sociable person, she didn't have a girlfriend she could talk to. In her cell phone she had the number of her therapist, whom she hadn't been to see for many months. Lirit thought that she didn't want to open up the subject of her mother's death with herself, or with anyone else either, including her therapist.

Mandy had found the therapist for her in Smuts Avenue in Tel Aviv, and she had gone to her about ten times over the period of a year. She and her mother never referred to the therapist by her name, but would say, "the therapist from Smuts Avenue."

There was no doubt that Lirit herself felt that she had undergone a significant amputation, but she didn't confront reality head on. She said to herself that she would wait for her father and face it then, because in the circumstances, when even Dael had disappeared from the picture, she was afraid of falling apart. If Lirit had had a support in her short life, it was her mother.

In Dizengoff Center they had installed spiral escalators,

of the kind her father had invented, and Lirit felt she had entitlement to wander round the place, go up and down the escalators and in and out of the shops, to her heart's content.

On the way home with all her shopping bags, the taxi driver charged extra for the weight. Lirit felt ridiculous when he stopped outside the entrance and helped her to empty the taxi of all the shopping bags bearing the names of top designers. It took her fifteen minutes to get it all inside, in several rounds.

Inside the house the shopping bags took up a large area of the living room. Suddenly she felt nauseous, as she always did after she had done something superfluous, or not particularly necessary.

It was a Thursday, and she only had until tomorrow to find storage solutions for all her new clothes. When Dael came home for the weekend, she wanted all the goodies to be organized in the closets, as if they had always been there.

She cut the labels off the garments and threw them into the blue recycling bin in their garbage room, together with the paper bags. At the same time she collected all her *shanti* clothes from the Shlomi era, all kinds of *salwars*, sandals made from recycled leather, and secondhand clothes from India and Thailand, and packed them into eight big plastic bags, black and opaque.

Feeling guilty and upset she got into the Jacuzzi, and dripped in neroli oil, which had a label on it with writing in an unfamiliar hand, "For severe depression and healing wounds." The thirty-six shopping bags had really cost a lot of money, she said to herself, conscience stricken. But never mind, it was because of the grief.

AFTER THE JACUZZI, Lirit moved the black bags onto the porch of the triplex, in case her father suddenly showed up and asked what they were. She wouldn't have the courage to tell him the truth, and if he thought that she had started to get rid of her mother's clothes, he might be angry.

In any case he wasn't in such great shape at the moment; there was no point in getting into an argument with him now.

A few hours after the darkness deepened, and under its cover, she stood and threw the bags full of her old clothes off the porch, and they landed on the evergreen vegetation of the place. Afterward she went downstairs, picked them up one by one, and loaded them into the car.

Lirit didn't have far to drive before she found, in a neighborhood next to Telba-North, a collection bin for the needy, as noted on the side in letters clearly visible during the day, but invisible in the dark. For a long time she stood there and hoisted the big bags into the bin, until it was full to overflowing and she had to cram them in by force. She left the last bag by the side of the bin, and drove away.

She called Inquiries for the number of the electronic answering service of arrivals and departures at Ben-Gurion Airport, and wrote down all the arrival times of the big airlines that seemed reasonable to her.

PART III

1

GRUBER'S FLIGHT TO NEW YORK (JFK), AND FROM THERE TO Israel by El Al, was supposed to depart from Ithaca at six in the morning. At four forty-five Bahat woke him up, full of a joy the likes of which she had not known for a long time. A new era was opening. She was smartly dressed and made up, as if she was going out on a date, not driving to the quaint Ithaca airport.

So intense was her desire for Gruber to be gone that if she could have she would have flown him as far as Cyprus herself. Anything further than that she considered too dangerous.

She went up to the guest room where the guest was sleeping. The door was slightly ajar. She went in and called his name three or four times. When he didn't answer she came closer to the bed and even shook him, until he opened red eyes and said,

"Leave me alone, Bahat. Let me sleep."

"But your plane leaves at six. You have to go to the airport now. Come on, your suitcase is already in the trunk, I packed it myself. You fell asleep with your clothes on, so just get up and freshen yourself up and let's go. I found you a new toothbrush because I already packed yours."

"Five more minutes," said Gruber and went back to sleep.

Five minutes passed, and the story repeated itself until in the end Gruber sat up in bed with his eyes closed and sighed bitterly. Bahat thought he was groaning in pain and her heart went out to him.

"My dear," she said gently, "we undergo hard things in our lives. But we have to carry on. You must get up," she bent over him. "You have responsibilities."

"Yes, but there's no funeral, right? So I'll leave on the next flight. It isn't a tragedy. You know why?" He stood up, his eyes still closed, and his clothes smelling of alcohol, sweat, and other smells banned by international conventions. "Because the tragedy has already happened. The tragedy is behind us."

"You have a responsibility to your children to be united with them in your grief. To seclude yourselves."

"What business is it of yours in the first place?" asked Gruber in a kind of illumination and he opened his eyes for a minute. "Where do you get off telling me to seclude myself. Why should anybody in the world tell *me* how to behave in a time of trouble? What's important is where I can go on sleeping now. All the bedclothes are stinking. I need fresh clothes. I sweated like a pig last night."

"If you like I'll change your bedclothes right now," said Bahat on her way out of the room.

"Why change the bedclothes!" Gruber called after her. "Just bring me some dry tracksuit. And hurry up, I don't want to wake up, or I won't be able to get back to sleep." He sat down and closed his eyes again.

"Okay," said Bahat and hurried to the walk-in closet. She still didn't get where the Israeli was going with this, or maybe he was simply broken up and he wasn't going anywhere. She came back with an Adidas tracksuit. Gruber was already waiting for her half naked, having thrown his dirty shirt onto the floor like a boy.

"Give it to me," he said. He put on the tracksuit, and went back to sleep.

Bahat thought it was a question of aftereffect and delayed reaction. At the most, he would miss this flight and leave tomorrow. The airport was open tomorrow too. It wasn't the end of the world. Nevertheless, she wasn't cut out for decadent enigmas, but for charging ahead.

She sat down in the living room and waited. There was nothing more for her to do. There was no longer any need or point to escaping into the spider research. She went to her Jewish bookshelf and took down a volume of the Talmud and tried to read it, but she had zero focus.

At one o'clock in the afternoon, Irad came downstairs and apologized profusely. He said that he was simply no longer capable of distinguishing between what was important and what wasn't important. Bahat said that it was only human to behave strangely in situations of distress, and that it was impossible to expect everyone to be at their best every day, what he had done yesterday was enough, he was definitely head and shoulders above the average person.

She put his coffee down in front of him.

"How about a snack? Something sweet?" she asked.

"No thank you," he replied, and after a minute he said:

"I've come to a conclusion."

"Yes?" asked Bahat curiously.

"I'm not going back to Israel. At least not soon. I need more time before I go back there. I'm staying here in the meantime, if you don't mind. I really like your bedroom and the direction of the view; it faces east, right?"

"Yes."

"Then let's change, just for a few days. You get the morning sun. I don't want to get rickets. My room doesn't have a serious window."

Bahat wanted to react to the criticism and tell him that she didn't see any need for enlarging the window in the guest room since she hardly had any guests, and certainly not for long enough to make them worry about the shortcomings of the room.

"I'd like to stay in your room for a few days," said Gruber, "and for you to sleep in the room you gave me. Just for a few days . . ."

"But your children, and the terror suit project—what do you call it—the TESU."

"My children," he said and wrung his hands. "They have already received the blow. And now they're ready to absorb the next one. I won't let them know. They'll understand for themselves. This way they'll get it into their heads gradually. Not in a boom. I won't answer the phone, and *you'll* say that I've gone and you don't know where. No," he paused, "that's too dramatic, I will speak to them. If they ring, I'll talk to them."

"And the project?"

"Last night I sent the defense minister an email. That there's news, there's a breakthrough, and the critics and slanderers can shut their mouths. I didn't go into detail, so he wouldn't take the credit at my expense. I said I was on my way. That doesn't mean I have to be there to kowtow to him in two days' time. Let him crawl a bit himself. There's no question about it, Bahat, it's a great achievement."

For the first time she noticed that for a while now he had been calling her by her first name, and it pleased her because he pronounced the *h* so beautifully, with a lot of aspiration, and didn't turn her into Bay-hat like the Americans did.

He went on:

"All you have to do, *Bahat*, is to understand that this is the reaction of a very sensitive man, whose ship of life has reached the gulf of oblivion. I myself haven't yet taken in this duality, that on the one hand you've given me the data, and on the other hand my wife is dead and I'm a *widower*, can you believe it? Me? A widower? I feel as if the laws of physics have changed."

He rested his brow on his hand, and what could Bahat say?

After a silence he added:

"I think that five hundred dollars a week, including food and laundry, would be very reasonable. Can you wheel my suitcase back in from the car?"

Bahat froze in her place, still confused.

"Irad Gruber, you are a very unusual person," she said in the end, taut as a spring. Her nervous system reacted before she did. "Who else is like you? And who do you really care about?"

"Obviously I care about my children and my work. And my poor wife. And myself of course. But I can't move until I restart, do you understand?"

"And you think," she said and began pacing round the room, "that you have some special right to an absolutely deluxe restart, while others can restart in the heart of their distress?"

"I don't think I have the right. I simply know that there's no other way for me to get over my wife's death except by staying a few more days in the diaspora and not jumping right back into the fray in Israel. In the past months I've been working so hard, and the pressure I'm under could give me a stroke on the spot, and then what? Who would take care of everybody? I'll restart, and then I'll check all the errors and fix them one by one, on a linear model. And you can simply relate to me as if I'm the pilot who fell into your house, and you're the little princess who stays with him during the difficult moments until he fixes the plane."

Bahat blushed. He'd read Saint-Exupéry?

He asked for a towel and went into the bathroom. Bahat quickly called Professor Propheta in Berkeley, and caught him on his cell phone. She apologized for turning him out, and told him about what was going on in her house. Now she understood that it was a critical mistake. She should have let him stay, and he would have helped her. They would have been two against one, now she was absolutely alone facing—

"The enemy," said Propheta and sniggered. "I'm telling you, every Israeli is an occupier. That's what they do. And now, seriously, listen Bahat, he's lost it temporarily, two or three days and then he'll leave. His wife died. He can't afford to go on acting like a freaked-out kid stuck in India forever."

He advised her not to do anything radical for the time being, like bringing in the police, or calling someone in the consulate in New York. The whole thing seemed to him like an aberration caused by grief.

"It's a pity we can't put him to sleep and lock him in a suitcase," said Bahat.

"Yes," said Propheta and chuckled. "Interesting how stupidity and genius can exist side by side in the same person."

"Tell that to your students," said Bahat and put the phone down. Afterward, worried, she went out to her car and wheeled the suitcase back in.

EVERY HALF HOUR or so she went to check if the temporary consent signed by Rabbi Shlesinger was still in the drawer, and that the barrier separating her from society had indeed fallen. At the official ordination, which would take place in New York on the twentieth of the following month, she would have to make a speech. And she would make it. She planned to talk about the first woman rabbi in history, Deborah the wife of Lapidoth, and to say that she was following in her footsteps and nothing more. She felt like being modest because she wanted those responsible to know that not only had she done something for the State of Israel that the time had not yet come to reveal, the importance of which was beyond doubt, but that she was also someone who knew how to move aside when necessary. Moving aside when necessary was in Bahat's eyes a noble virtue, and when she imagined herself moving aside, for example for the sake of her daughters, she always thought of the great sage Rashi's mother and how she moved aside and was saved from the pogrom by the opening up of the magic wall of Worms.

IN THE DISTANT Telba-North, Lirit was already beginning to wonder why there was no word yet from her father, and she even had a touching telephone conversation on the subject with Dael. Dael too didn't understand what was going on, but he didn't tell his sister he suspected their father of going AWOL. He expressed the hope that nothing had happened to him. Lirit told him she had checked with the Defense Ministry, and they told her there that he had contacted them by email and said that he was late because he was sitting shivah for his wife in Ithaca.

"Sitting shivah?"

"That's what they said he said."

But about an hour after the conversation with her brother, Lirit received a call from America. It was their father, and this time he gave her a phone number, he was very warm, he even called her "my love," and she immediately melted because he had never called her that before.

Lirit asked him if everything was all right, and he said that obviously nothing was all right, and Lirit was surprised, she never knew that her father was so attached to her mother, and even if he was, it was a strange way to treat her death.

And then she did something that her mother would have done if she had been alive, or if she had been in her place. Lirit asked to speak to Bahat.

IRAD REACHED OUT and handed the phone wordlessly to his hostess.

"What?" asked Bahat.

"My daughter wants to talk to you."

She took the receiver and said,

"Hello?"

Lirit introduced herself—very politely, clearly a well brought-up girl, the mother had done a good job. Lirit brought Bahat up to date briefly on what Lirit already knew that Bahat knew, and asked her opinion on what was happening.

"What do you mean?" asked Bahat.

"How is he acting?"

"Listen—"

"Is it difficult for you to talk? Can he hear?"

"Every word," said Bahat.

"Can't you distance yourself from him a bit? *Our* cordless

phones work over a distance of several hundred feet. How about yours?"

Bahat went down to the ground floor and said:

"I really don't know. I don't think that your father can take a long journey. That's clear. I'll have to look after him for a while."

"Is he eating?" asked Lirit.

"Very little. Yesterday he ate soup, and with that he did me a favor. He left half of it. And today a tuna sandwich in the morning, and then he told me he threw it up."

"Is he drinking?"

"Coffee nonstop."

"No, I'm asking about alcohol."

"I don't keep alcohol in the house, ever since my girls were living here."

"I understand," said Lirit. "Okay, look," she said, "he gave me a phone number, and I'd like to verify it."

The number Lirit read out to her bore no resemblance to her telephone number.

"The question is whether he's aware," said Lirit, and there was a note of profound concern in her voice.

"I don't know what to tell you," said Bahat, "the situation is confusing me too and disrupting my life. Does he have a boss you can talk to? People that can shake him out of it? Friends? A brother? Someone."

"Of course he has. He's a person with a lot of friends. But let's wait, because I don't want to get him into trouble, if it's a crisis that will blow over soon then the whole world doesn't have to—"

"I very much hope so," said Bahat.

2

"IF THERE'S SUCH A THING AS REINCARNATION," SAID DAEL to his sister over the phone, "then in my next incarnation I want to be a tree. But not a cypress. Nothing so exposed. Or you know what, I'd prefer something inanimate. Like a piece of pipe. Something completely useless. And that way I'll know," the soldier sniggered, "that anyone who's my friend is a real friend, because I'm just a pipe rusting in the desert . . ." he laughed. "You don't know what a night I had, Lirit, the world's worst—"

But Dael was wasting airtime on his sister because she too was very upset. In her last phone conversation with their father, at midnight on the US East Coast, he had dropped a bomb. He told her that he had *fallen in love* with Bahat, deeply, desperately. It was stronger than he was, it had shaken him to the foundations, and he didn't know what to do.

Lirit asked her father if Bahat was in love with him as well, and he said sadly that he was the last thing in the world that interested Bahat. Lirit wondered if she should have a frank talk with Bahat, but she thought that it would be a betrayal of her father, and she decided against it. The father said to his daughter that Bahat was now in a place from which "she was looking outward," to what was beyond loneliness, to people, action, movement, helping others. That she was about to become a Reform rabbi and she couldn't wait to get started.

Gruber suffered from a disorder of excessive talkativeness, and now, on the phone with Dael, there was no stopping his daughter either. She grabbed the floor from her brother, in the middle of the dialogue of the deaf, and explained to him that as she understood it Bahat was sick of staying at home, and all she wanted was to get out, out of Ithaca to New York, to Mississippi, to Utah, to roam the length and breadth of the USA, to meet people, convert here, marry a Jewish couple there, see the world, live on a very busy schedule, with no time for anything between one thing and the next but getting to that next thing. Just imagine, she's going to be a rabbi! Our father has fallen in love with a rabbi, and claims he's never felt like this about a woman before and he has to make the most of his new situation! Such happiness!

THE NEW INFORMATION did not succeed in really penetrating Dael's mind. He was preoccupied with the event of late last night. If only his mother had been alive, and he could have told her what had happened, she would have been properly astonished.

Now all that was left him was to imagine himself telling her, and her murmuring intently: That's terrible! That's shocking, Dael! That's incredible, Dael! Mainly she would have repeated his name again and again, Dael, Dael. She was the one who had chosen this name. Gruber had chosen Lirit's name, and she had insisted on Dael's.

They had an assassination. Everything proceeded according to plan until the moment when Dael shot at the center of the mass, saw the guy taking the bullet and not falling, shot again, and saw him taking the bullet and not falling, until in the end he fell. In the meantime they were being shot at, and he and his friends ran under fire to confirm the kill, and saw that the target was padded round the chest with a belt of Yellow Pages from every area of the country.

Dael had almost been killed by the shots fired at them. Do you understand? To die right after you, mother?

This was why he preferred to be a useless piece of pipe, etc.

At the end of this imaginary conversation he called Aya Ben-Yaish, in the hope that she would listen to him, and say something, maybe that it was a miracle he was alive, because it really was a miracle. Aya Ben-Yaish was not available, and Dael went to continue his breadth reading of Scott Fitzgerald, Homer, a biography of Moshe Dayan, and Primo Levi.

AT THE END of her morning conversation with her brother, Lirit felt a great emptiness. She didn't have Mandy's talent for throwing the right slogans into the air and bringing the man home in the space of a few hours.

Later on she raced north on the coastal road. The traffic was less heavy now than at eight, and she, unlike her mother, had no intention of getting up at the crack of dawn and arriving at the factory at half past six, seven. Those days were over. On the radio too they said that the northbound traffic was proceeding unimpeded, but that at some junction, not connected to her, oil had been spilled on the road.

Why had he fallen in love all of a sudden? What was really going on there? In the end, contrary to her previous decision, she called Bahat, even though over there it was maybe five in the morning. And the latter answered immediately, and listened to the young Israeli, who was trying to preach to her from a distance, and then Bahat said, "Honey, your father and I have only spent two nights together. I wanted to cheer him up, and I'm a woman too. Believe me, we both needed it. Your mother hasn't had sex with him for years. He told me. Did you know? Did she have a lover?"

"Can I talk to him?" asked Lirit, who simply couldn't believe her ears.

"He's sleeping."

"When he wakes up, tell him to call the factory urgently, or me on my cell phone!" she said, and only when she arrived at Nighty-Night, she noticed that the left-hand outside mirror had been ripped off the car.

SHE PARKED the big Buick next to the Singer technician's Fiesta. What could you do? Class divisions were class divisions. The commotion at the entrance to the factory signaled anarchy. After she entered the air-conditioned interior, and the beads of sweat on her forehead stopped forming pools, she saw Carmela Levy trying to get the panic-stricken seamstresses to calm down. Only the Singer technician was nowhere to be seen, and she concluded that he was busy oiling the machines. She would introduce advanced technology, for God's sake! Far more efficient sewing machines had already been invented; she had leafed through the textile journal Mandy subscribed to and seen sophisticated models there. She wondered how much they cost.

Carmela hushed the girls, and Lirit realized that Carmela had organized them under her wing, and she was sheltering them.

Although this wasn't the first time she had visited the factory after the death of the boss, the girls' faces looked distraught due to the uncertainty, and rightly so. It seemed that in spite of the facade that everything was under control (by intuition or from television, she knew that she had to show authority), it was clear to the workers that she too didn't know what she wanted.

"Assembly in the canteen in half an hour," she said and went up to Mandy's office. Carmela asked if she wanted her to come upstairs to the offices with her, and Lirit understood that the first thing she had to do was to fire this woman, and she said to her, "No need."

No hand but Mandy's, or somebody authorized by her, touched the office and the special things she kept there in glass-fronted cabinets, such as the collection of dolls from all over the world. Carmela was the only person she permitted to dust her delicate collections, for some of the knickknacks were breakable, or broken and put together again. The collection of dolls from all over the world Mandy had inherited from her mother Audrey Greenholtz, the founder of the factory.

When Lirit was little, her mother had strictly forbidden her to touch these dolls, as if they were cursed or something. Afterward there was a period when the curse was lifted, and Mandy let her, but two years later when she was at about the age of fifteen, madam had decided that Lirit's hands had become clumsy due to the surge of hormonal energy, and she was relegated to her previous status with regard to the collections.

But now she was dead, and Lirit sat on her executive chair and adjusted it to suit her. The air-conditioner was set at freezing, the way Mandy liked it, the computer was dark, and when Lirit pressed enter, to see what was on the screen, she was surprised to see a picture of herself and her brother as children, sitting and eating popsicles on the beach. It was very moving, but Lirit had no time for such luxuries, and she took a pen and paper and started to write down notes for her speech.

She didn't want to lie, and so she noted to herself to say that she didn't want to lie or mislead any of the loyal workers, but there was no doubt that they were in a period of uncertainty and it was impossible to know what was going to happen. Only six days had passed since Mandy had passed away. She crossed out Mandy and wrote Amanda. And she continued that she herself had not yet started to digest what had happened and why, and she had no, she repeated, she had *no* detailed plans with regard to the factory and the future of its workers.

This, in fact, was the gist of what she had to say. And when she said it in the canteen, some of the girls burst into tears and others talked about compensation. She repeated that the situation was not clear, and that they all had to understand that she had received a harsh blow, and she did not yet have the strength either to carry on from where her mother left off, or to set out on a new path.

Somebody pointed out that this wasn't what she had said a few days ago on the phone. They reminded her that she said they had to continue on Mandy's path, and Lirit admitted that she had said so because that was what people always said, but they didn't mean it literally. It was impossible to swim in the same river twice, she said, and stressed again that she didn't know what was going to happen. They had to understand that there wasn't only a crisis in the textile industry, there was also a crisis in Nighty-Night, and it was impossible to jump straight into a resolution of the crisis before the crisis had spoken its last word.

The women had no idea what she was talking about. They were resentful. They had unemployed husbands and families to feed. They couldn't live like this. But she raised the banner of uncertainty again and the need for everyone, including herself, to go with the flow of this uncertainty for the time being.

ON THE WAY BACK from Netanya she wondered what she was really going to do with the pajama factory. What changes should she introduce? Should she renovate, or continue the tradition? Was it tradition or stagnation? And what about what she had once thought could be a big hit today: pajamas for babies and toddlers made from organic cotton?

Clearly people in the top 10 percent would buy them for the use of their offspring, and maybe the 30 or 40 percents below that too. People would buy them as gifts for baby showers too, if the babies were dear to them.

Yes, why not? Lirit mused, and nearly missed the turnoff, but managed to change course in time, though fortunately for her there were no traffic cops or cameras in the vicinity. Pajamas from organic cotton! She began racking her brains for slogans for a future advertising campaign. And perhaps not only for infants? She expanded her plans. For all ages! Yes. Why discriminate against the parents? Lirit let her thoughts range far and wide: first she would put out a line of pajamas for infants from organically grown cotton, and later on the same thing for all ages, under the slogan, "Why shortchange the parents?" She already had a vision of what an advertising campaign for both items at once would look like: Give them to your children and also to Mom and Dad and Granny and Grandpa, who gave their all to their children . . .

Today, said Lirit to herself, people take great care of their bodies and their health because of the security situation in the world, not only in Israel. The more the security situation deteriorates, the more people will invest in sporting appliances, vitamins, nutritional supplements, organic vegetables, and organic cotton.

She remembered that a year ago she had been on a shopping expedition with Mandy at the up-market Ramat Aviv mall. They both tried on bras, and nothing felt comfortable. Mandy said that all the bra manufacturers should be forced to use organic cotton in their products so that they wouldn't scratch people.

"You and I are actually in the same position as far as gravity is concerned," Mandy said to her on the same occasion, having just undergone breast-lifting surgery.

After they had each bought two bras, and they went down to the underground parking garage, they heard people in the elevator talking about some new outrage that had taken place an hour ago. Mandy was stressed out until she extracted the information vital to her from the passengers in the elevator: the casualties were civilian.

"I don't even care about civilians anymore," she said when they got out of the elevator, "only about soldiers. You know?" she looked at her nodding daughter. "About children and babies I don't feel anything anymore. I don't want to know anything about them. Not four year olds and not one year olds. Or one month. But when a soldier dies, I die. I think about his mother. Naturally after I find out that I'm not his mother. If it happens to my son, I'll kill myself on the spot. I'm sure a lot of mothers feel the same way. My life's not worth living without Dael."

"And without me is your life worth living?"

"You'll manage very well without me," said Mandy and pressed the remote that opened with a shriek the car whose beauty stood out even among the cars of the shoppers at the Ramat Aviv mall.

"And Daddy?"

"Your father doesn't need anyone," said Mandy and made her way through the parking garage to the exit to Einstein Street.

She dawdled a bit, because it was their old neighborhood, and they even passed their old house at 44 Tagore Street, and sat and looked for a moment at the place where they used to live, and then they continued driving east on Keren Kayemet Avenue.

While Lirit was remembering all the above, Bahat was trying to call her, but Lirit didn't hear the ring because she was playing a tape very loudly to herself. The radio had been tuned to a station playing Hebrew songs, but Lirit had soon put a stop to that.

Accordingly, Bahat was obliged to remain with the facts seething inside her, without an outlet in Israel.

She wanted to complain to Lirit, or anyone, about the phenomenon of Gruber, and she wanted to demand that Lirit come and get him. No, enough was enough, she couldn't stand him anymore.

It was the little things that broke her. Gruber left the bathroom in a disgusting state, even if he only went in to brush his teeth and comb his hair. He behaved as if seven chambermaids were following him around wherever he went. And in the toilet, the way he urinated annoyed her. It was many years since she had had to clean leftover urine from the toilet bowl. And now that she had to do it again, she felt great annoyance.

The man, it turned out, raised the toilet seat, but failed to lower it again, and sometimes, albeit rarely, he didn't even take the trouble to raise it, and this, in her opinion, was the height of chutzpah. Who did he think he was, an animal? He finished the toilet paper and didn't change the roll. And he still had the nerve to argue that Mandy had allowed him not to change it, because he had trouble with the spring. What kind of an argument was that? Was that the way he behaved with his wife, or did he think that his wife's laws were valid for her as well?

She began to detest the guest more and more, and he, for his part, grew more and more demanding and dependent, and was convinced that everything he did stemmed from his outburst of feelings for Bahat. All this was not at all what the enthusiastic Reform rabbi had in mind. The prayer shawl, and the big skullcap, which she hadn't yet decided whether to wear or not, were in a drawer in her closet, folded up.

For three nights now she had been sleeping in the rarely used guest room, while he lay sprawled on her comfortable bed. He sweated so much at night, because of the objective situation, that she was obliged to change his sheets every day. He asked to be involved in the choice of sheets, because he claimed that Bahat's bed linen was depressing.

She was also repelled by his negligence, by his failure to return to Israel with the information she had given him in order to continue his experiments with the requisite urgency. Every day that passed claimed more victims who could have been saved if he hadn't thought only of himself, and she patted herself on the shoulder, noting that her thoughts were becoming more and more moral.

From time to time he said to her, "I love you," in English. And also "I love you very much." It was impossible to tell anything from these declarations because they were in blatant contradiction to his behavior. It was clear to her that he had completely freaked out, and she only hoped that his love would be short-lived, like that of the Hispanic Salazar: two weeks of sensual intoxication, and after that as if nothing had happened, coolness lacking in tension, but empathy and outstanding efficiency.

Bahat had a theory that her latest discoveries about the silk protein were made possible by spare libido, at least on her part. As for Salazar, she had no idea what motivated him, but his ideas were brilliant.

In the end she despaired of her attempts to contact Lirit and she decided to take things into her own hands. As long as the seven days of mourning for his wife lasted (Gruber began the shivah from the moment he was informed of her death), she would show restraint. After that she would assert herself.

3

ON THE NIGHT BETWEEN THE SIXTH AND SEVENTH DAY of mourning, Gruber wet the bed. Since Bahat was sleeping in the guest room she was spared the direct experience, although he did call her in the middle of the night to change the sheets.

As far as Bahat was concerned this was a sign to phone a psychiatrist and request an urgent home visit. The effort of persuading the squatter to leave the house and go to the psychiatrist's office seemed to her an investment of energy that she needed for herself and which she wasn't about to put at Gruber's disposal, not even out of philanthropy.

She opened the Ithaca Yellow Pages and looked up the number of the well-known medical center of the town. There she obtained the name of a psychiatrist who she assumed, like every other psychiatrist in the world, received private patients as well. She spoke to his secretary at his official place of work and found a pretext for getting his home and cell phone numbers out of her.

The man's name was Bill Stanton. A healthy instinct led her to the conclusion that Gruber should on no account be seen by a female psychiatrist. Stanton said that he would drop in on his way to work. No, he didn't take money for the first consultation, only for the second. She asked if a home visit had to be paid for anyway, and he said that in this case too he only took money for the second visit. This was his conception, he said and laughed, he believed that it was enough for a person to have to see a psychiatrist, he didn't have to pay for it as well.

But McPhee was suspicious of this argument because she had heard of the new community founded by one thousand of the twenty thousand whites (20,893 white citizens, who constituted 71.3 percent of the population of the town). Anyone in Ithaca could be a member of the new community, even if he was one of the 460 Puerto Ricans in the town, or one of the 125 Vietnamese. Whether he was man over eighteen of any race and color (13,433), or a woman over eighteen of any race and color (13,149).

This community had set itself the goal of increasing the goodness inherent in all human beings, of all sectors and genders, and it was called the Goodwill Community. All the members happened to be whites who lived on the outskirts of the town and provided themselves with all the services they required not for money, but through a system of barter. And as for the rest of the inhabitants of Ithaca, whether they belonged to the 1,555 Hispanics (or Latino-Americans, according to the accepted usage of the day), or the 1,965 Afro-Americans, or Chinese by origin (1,659), or of any other race (356), they were all entitled to significant reductions. They enjoyed the services of the Goodwill Community for a symbolic fee, which was itself donated to charity.

The fact that Dr. Bill Stanton turned out to be a member of the Goodwill Community bothered Bahat, because she was afraid she would hesitate to ask him for all kinds of extras on his home visit.

McPhee wasn't prepared for charitable freebies. She wanted an accurate diagnosis, but at the same time as comprehensive as possible.

DR. BILL STANTON arrived the same day. He spoke to Gruber in his room for a long time, and afterward he came out to Bahat, who was waiting in suspense in the hallway.

He told her that he was hesitating between a diagnosis of recurrent major depression with symptoms of compulsive behavior (including the symptom of his falling in love with her), and post-traumatic stress disorder, in which case his depression, and all his bizarre behavior, including the falling in love, were only a side effect of the disorder.

He had no doubt that Gruber was a borderline case, and in view of his other doubts regarding the diagnosis, he asked for permission to use the telephone in order to consult a colleague, since the medication for the two conditions was different.

"Medication?" asked Bahat.

"Yes."

He spoke for about five minutes on the phone and then he explained:

"We try one kind of medication, and if it works, we continue, and if it doesn't, it's a sign that it's the second possibility, and in this way we arrive at the right medication, in the hope that it is indeed right. In any case, it will take two or three weeks, or even more, to see what works, and judging by what works we'll know what's wrong with him."

"Dr. Stanton," said Bahat with all the restraint at her command, "this man is an Israeli. He isn't an American citizen. He has no visa to stay here. Who knows if he even has medical insurance. His presence here is actually illegal. He came here to give me information. I received the information. He can go back to his own country. And as for the trauma, it's simple: his wife died a little over a week ago, and that's the whole trauma."

"The trauma predates the death of his wife," said Stanton. "This isn't a fresh trauma. I can recognize a fresh trauma when I see one."

"I can recognize a fresh trauma too," said Bahat, red in the face with rage, "this person simply went crazy in front of my eyes and he needs to be committed to an institution! He has two children waiting for him in Israel. Two motherless children. They don't understand what's going on. Give him an injection and we'll send him back to where he came from."

Stanton laughed.

"Mrs. McPhee, we don't use those methods here. And speaking personally I don't think I could do it either," he added. And then he said quietly, "As far as I'm concerned, as soon as I turn my back you can throw him into the street. Where he'll be arrested for vagrancy. There are policemen everywhere now. There was fighting among the Natives (there are 289 Native Americans in Ithaca) and the police are patrolling all the streets. I'm sure he'll be arrested for vagrancy, and I have no doubt that in his condition he doesn't really remember your address . . ."

At this point he raised his voice again,

"So what do we have here, Mrs. McPhee? We have denial of reality—what it stems from has yet to be ascertained."

"And if the pills don't take effect in three weeks?"

"Then we'll try the post-traumatic treatment."

"Because of the death of his wife?" Bahat insisted.

"No," said Stanton. "He reacted to his wife's death by falling obsessively in love with you."

"I understand," said Bahat. "In other words, six weeks maximum?"

"More or less," said the doctor.

"I don't believe it," said Bahat, with tears in her eyes. "I don't understand."

Stanton decided to invest a little more in this woman; he laid his hand on her shoulder and said:

"My bet is that he's post-traumatic, but I want to eliminate the depression first. And then get him onto a post-traumatic protocol. The medication for depression works faster than the post-trauma medication, and we should try to shorten the period of uncertainty as much as possible."

"Interesting," murmured McPhee.

Stanton continued, "He told me that they recently moved into a new neighborhood. That's the trauma. There's a certain tree there, a type of palm, that he detests. He prefers their old house, but he and his wife, the one who died, have already sold it."

"So what do we do now?" she asked. "On the twentieth of next month I have an ordination. It's a very serious ceremony. I have to prepare. I have to write a speech. He makes so much noise. I can't put up with it."

"I've already told you what I can suggest. Now I must go. There's no lack of trouble in the world."

He left.

BAHAT TRIED Lirit again, without success. She toyed with the idea of sending him out to buy bread in the hope that he would get lost. But on second thoughts she decided that she didn't want to endanger the special status she had gained in the eyes of Schlesinger, the Albany Reform rabbi. If this man wandered round outside, she was almost sure that with his extroversion, even Schlesinger would hear that he was still in America and understand that the Israelis had not yet made any use of the classified information, and then the whole loneliness-alleviating project would go down the drain.

She dropped onto the living-room sofa in despair. From Gruber's room on the second floor she heard Edith Bunker's voice screeching "Ar-chie!"—and the intruder's hoarse wheezing laugh.

She switched on the television and stared at the National Geographic channel. Yes, she would be better off letting the anarchy rage around her, and watching something more organized, such as the nesting of the condor.

She fell asleep for a few minutes, and when she woke up she saw Irad standing and looking at her. He was unshaven and even from a distance reeked of every possible kind of odor, perhaps he had even brought some of them with him from Israel. He said, this time without a hint of demand,

"I'm hungry."

"Eat something."

"I don't know how to cook for myself, but I'll keep you company while you cook. That's what I used to do in the old house. Sit in the kitchen and talk to Mandy. There was room in the kitchen there."

"And in the new house there isn't any?"

214

"There isn't any room, and Mandy isn't there either," he said and sank into despair.

"Omelet or scrambled egg?" asked Bahat with forced brightness and made for the kitchen.

"Scrambled," said Irad.

4

LIRIT TRIED ON HER MOTHER'S BURGUNDY BRA. SHE wanted to see if Mandy was right when she said in the Ramat Aviv mall that from the point of view of gravity they were both equal. Mandy's bra was too big for her. Her mother was mistaken. She had only had a breast lift, not a breast reduction.

Now she was about to set out for a very important meeting on Kibbutz Kissufim, and she dressed with an elegance suitable to Israel, without too much joie de vivre. After exhaustive inquiries, in the course of which she had encountered the usual wall of silence encountered by people trying to clarify something (it being human nature to retreat when faced by the possibility of clarification, for all kinds of reasons of survival), she had reached a certain Oron de Bouton, who for some years had been growing organic cotton of the Pima variety on Kibbutz Kissufim, by sub-surface drip irrigation.

It took her a long time to understand what was meant by sub-surface drip irrigation, but the minute she understood she thought she was a genius.

Now she was on her way to find what it meant, in terms of threads and money, to get into the market of organic cotton.

Let the workers in the factory carry on making pajamas for the ultra-Orthodox sector until further notice, she said to herself. That was all for the best. And in the meantime she herself would carry on going ahead with her inquiries. It actually suited her for her father to be having some scene with himself and someone else as crazy as he was, who had also spent years of her life with spiders. Now she, Lirit, was truly free. It was ridiculous what her father was doing with his life when he could be sitting at home and making a decent living from regular textile, without all the sensations and headaches. After all, he wasn't an idiot, he must know that the safest thing today was to go for textile that already existed, which he had at home.

Lirit was only twenty-two, and look how much experience of life she already had. There was no need to go to America, she added to herself, it was enough to go to Kibbutz Kissufim.

Even though she didn't say so to herself in so many words, Lirit had been wounded to the depths of her soul by her father's failure to return to Israel at such a difficult time, and she didn't know if she could ever forgive him. There were probably cultures where they stoned people for this kind of thing without thinking twice. With all due respect to him and his Israel Prize, this time he had gone too far. She wasn't going to forgive him.

Lirit had already found an outlet for her anger in the poor seamstresses at Nighty-Night. She took advantage of the atmosphere of anxiety surrounding them, and threw her weight around like a true autocrat, not of these times. Her mother would no doubt have been proud of her. Perhaps it was in her DNA.

And anyway, why shouldn't they be afraid? What was she supposed to do about it? Life isn't a picnic, Mandy would warn her whenever she was happy. She too was afraid of upsetting the status quo, especially if it was working well, but the status quo was so boring, and she knew that if she wanted to love this place (i.e. Nighty-Night), she was going to have to march it ahead. In the first place, change its name to something more up-to-date, transfer the production to China, which was several times cheaper than Turkey, and yes, let a large part of the workers go, with or without mercy. Instead of the fired workers, she would bring in ambitious young girls with gel and tattoos, graduates of the Shenkar Textile Design School, or talented foreigners, who had all kinds of weird ideas on subjects she had never heard of because with old Shlomi from Brosh on the border of Te'ashur she had stagnated. Now she wanted to get back into the swing of things.

The workers at Nighty-Night weren't living on a cloud either, and they already knew that a big change was about to take place in their lives: perhaps they would join the ranks of the unemployed, and from there slide into the vicious cycle of poverty, from which it was very difficult to emerge.

Lirit thought that she deserved to be congratulated. Her mother died, and she didn't break. On the contrary. She was strong and she was coping very well. She gave herself "Very good" in a teacher's handwriting. She was doing everything. Bringing herself up-to-date while also going forward. Yes, indeed. In some sense, life was miraculous. From a disappointment to her parents, a nothing with a boyfriend twice her age—and now she could already admit to herself *boring*, so boring (someone who photographed floods and flowers, with cameras and lenses that nobody dared to show in public anymore)—she had in a few days turned into the industrious and independent owner of a factory, without any additions to her beautiful back, with perfect shoulder blades like the ones her late mother had in her youth, and she was about to enter the Israeli pajama market with something amazing by any standard, organic cotton of the Pima variety grown by sub-surface drip irrigation on Kibbutz Kissufim of the United Kibbutz Movement.

It was going to be a huge success! Because what did people have left to rely on if not their pajamas. Let them too be made of natural materials. Let the stuff that enveloped their natural nightmares be natural too, and fit in with them harmoniously.

They started to play an irritating song on the radio. In general, Lirit didn't know three-quarters of the songs they played, which in her opinion was a shame and disgrace. She listened carefully to the words of the presenters introducing the songs she didn't know, as if she was sitting in a math class and had to remember the equations.

She switched to another station and the strains of a different band began to proudly review the new composition of her life. Suddenly she grew melancholy. What are you doing? You have set aside the whole truth and contented yourself with only a very curtailed version of it. You have just deliberately narrowed your world. In truth, your life is in ruins. Your dearly beloved mother will never return, not even to quarrel with you, and your father has lost his mind somewhere in northern New York.

Lirit addressed herself in the archaic language she had learned from her Grandmother Audrey, whose limited command of Hebrew was of an outdated variety.

Lirit would say something like "look" and her grandmother would say "pray look" and suchlike expressions. Lirit liked talking to herself in this language, because it gave her the feeling of security she used to have with her grandmother as a child.

Grandmother Audrey believed that in order to master a language, you had to first learn a few flowery phrases, and only after that the basics. In this way, even if you weren't fluent in the language, you learned the best of it, and even if you made mistakes, people would immediately understand how high you were aiming. Audrey Greenholtz repeated this to Lirit dozens of times, perhaps hundreds, until Lirit didn't have the strength for her anymore, and then either Lirit didn't answer her or she left the room in the middle of the repetitive speech.

Leave the future to its own devices! she accordingly said to herself. The time and tide will yet present themselves for you to set sail for New York to bring your father home. You have a million things to worry about before that.

Once again she banished from the arena of her thoughts the abandonment of her father and the death of her mother, on the grounds that she already knew the facts and she couldn't change the situation. It was all down to her, and therefore she had the moral legitimacy to put off grieving. Apart from which, Lirit preferred to think positive thoughts, and she went back to basking in her new status as the director of the pajama factory. If you looked at it in the long term, it was cruel but true, she had struck it lucky. Mandy's death had positive aspects too, in relation to Lirit's freedom of action and her personal growth. Her posture had improved a lot too. Suddenly her neck vertebrae were no longer at an angle to the rest of her spinal column, and her head didn't droop when she was walking.

Even her self-image had improved in the wake of compliments she had received from a top model she had met in Mikado, and also from her personal psychologist, Inbal Asherov, who she had gone to see on a one-off basis, and who had seemed very pleased with Lirit's progress.

She turned onto Route Six, the new toll road, and was impressed by its width and the fact that there wasn't much traffic on it at eleven in the morning. The meeting with the organic cotton grower Oron de Bouton was set to take place at noon at the entrance to Kibbutz Kissufim. It was relatively early and Lirit went over the lesson Mandy had tried for years to teach her and which she had rejected as if it was in a foreign language: the warp is vertical and the woof is horizontal. Fabrics are made of threads. Threads are made of fibers. The carding machine is the machine that combs the fibers. There's a cotton board, just like there's a poultry board.

5

"WHAT AN IDIOT THAT PSYCHIATRIST OF YOURS IS," SAID Irad and added salt to the *shakshuka* Bahat had made him instead of the scrambled egg. He had changed his mind a second before she broke the egg, and after she had served him the hot, bubbling dish of eggs and tomatoes, and he had sprinkled it with salt, he added:

"He's infantile. Who is *he* to diagnose *me*? Hey? You know what he said to me? No? So let me tell you, because it's about your elections. He told me that he was depressed, because the Democrats lost. I didn't know that the Democrats lost."

"The Democrats lost," said Bahat.

Gruber waved a scolding finger in the air.

"Your doctor, the psychiatrist, sounds to me like a very disturbed fellow. First of all, his appearance is nebulous and undefined. It's hard to tell if he's even handsome or ugly, he's so volatile. A person who doesn't take a fee for the initial consultation. Who's ever heard of such a thing? I don't think I'll even take the pills he prescribed me."

Bahat was horrified.

"What are you talking about? Bill Stanton? He's considered one of the finest in the entire state of New York! He graduated from Cornell with distinction! And he's from Ithaca," she concluded proudly.

"Enough already with that hubris," said Irad and buttered a slice of bread with which he quickly wiped his plate. Bahat looked at him and thought that he ate fast and a lot, and altogether he was costing her a fortune, and while they were both silent and he was eating, she calculated how much he had cost her since the moment of his arrival, including the massage and the meal at the French restaurant, and it came to over two thousand dollars. And of course, the five hundred dollars he had offered as a contribution to expenses, he had failed to mention again. Before she had time to take in this interim account another problem revealed itself: the medication. That too would no doubt cost a fortune. She was sorry, but she would have to ask him to share the expenses. She was sick and tired of all the egomaniacs in the world.

"My dear," Gruber suddenly addressed her with a confusing tenderness she had never come across before in a man of his age. "You shouldn't have called him in," he said, chewing another, extra, slice of bread and butter. "It's a waste of your time and effort. I can tell you myself what's wrong with me."

"Yes?" she said, wondering if he was going to tell her anything new.

"I was diagnosed three years ago by a senior psychologist at the Defense Ministry as borderline with a high level of organizing ability. Apart from that, I have a tendency to deep depression. Mandy, my wife, may she rest in peace, understood me very well. She understood that with geniuses, personality disorders, psychological disturbances, whatever you want to call it, are a must. The sensitivity and the ability to see the facts in a different light originate in the nervous system, which is also the first to suffer. What disorder do you suffer from?"

"Attention and concentration disorders and severe communication problems. Sometimes I stutter. That's why I don't give lectures as a rule. I begin on a subject, open parentheses and more parentheses, and forget what I'm supposed to be talking about. I'm not a sociable person," Bahat confessed and lowered her eyes.

"Do you take Ritalin?" asked Irad.

"Among other things."

"I don't take Ritalin, because it has side effects, especially if you're post-traumatic."

"So you are post-traumatic."

"Apart from my genius—on whose altar you'll find my nervous system—I am also post-traumatic, correct. I carry that on my back too," said Gruber, looking serious.

"And what's the trauma?"

"Moving houses," said Gruber quietly.

"Ah, yes. We've heard that before," said Bahat dismissively.

"It's the third most severe trauma in children. After death in the family and divorce."

"It happened to you as a child?" she asked. "I don't understand."

"No, it happened to me two years ago, when we moved to Tel Baruch North. It was a big blow. I didn't expect it to happen to someone of my age, in my position. Mandy said it would get better with time, she was in a bit of a shock herself . . ."

"Why? Where did you live before?"

"In Neve Avivim. 44 Tagore Street. You know it?"

"I don't know anything about those neighborhoods. What's the difference?"

"The difference? You've been stagnating here too long to understand the differences. You left when Neve Avivim had just been built, which is a long time ago. You haven't got a hope of getting to the bottom of the difference. In general, Neve Avivim and Tel Baruch North are as far apart as West from East. Aah," he sighed disconsolately. "Tel Baruch North is a place without a past, with tremendous difficulty in connecting to the present. That's how I feel anyway. And whoever did the landscape planning for the neighborhood did it without any heritage too. They filled the place with coconut palms! There are no butterflies, never mind honeysuckers. Or hedgehogs. There's no food chain. And lawns—there aren't any. Are there?" he tried to remember.

Bahat went to the sink with his plate and almost threw it in with the cutlery. She was really fed up. If he didn't take his pills, what was she going to do? She decided to call Propheta. Sometimes he gave excellent, spot-on advice.

"You know, Bahat," continued Gruber, in a more pleasant tone, as if he were a real-estate consultant with life experience. "It's not a good idea to buy a new apartment in a new location, with new infrastructure, new vegetation, new trees, new stairs, new everything. It's no good being the first in a certain place. It gives rise to anxiety. I like houses that have been lived in before. It's less frightening when you're not the first, when you're not supposed to determine anything, but there I feel a kind of obligation to the house itself, do you understand? As if I have to give it an ambience, do you understand?" he asked Bahat again.

"Every word," said the horrified Bahat.

"There's an overdose of newness there. The apartment, the

Jacuzzi, the doors, the neighborhood, the people, the neighbors, the shopping center, the shops in the shopping center, the moving stairs. How much have they already moved? I ask you. Has anyone checked the mileage? Ha?" He grunted in disgust. "I never had an anxiety attack in my life before, and since we moved there I have them all the time. I'd like to live in a house that's existed for two hundred years. Is that too much to ask?"

He shut up, but only for a minute.

"Have you ever had an anxiety attack, Bahat?" He turned to her and at the same time thought that he really did talk too much, Mandy was right.

Bahat didn't answer. Her face had begun to fall even before, as soon as he said that he wasn't going to take the pills, and now she looked weak, with a blue tinge to her skin.

"I don't like buying directly from the contractor, certainly not from the contractor's paper," the guest confessed loudly. "When there are previous occupants, you go into a place that *exists,* and you merge in quietly, like a side street with a main road. But when you move into a place like my apartment, you get an existential shock. And not only you. I'm sure that everyone who came to live there is in the same boat as me. I don't think any of them dared to put something secondhand into their apartments. At the beginning Mandy and I were completely crushed. In order to escape from the despair of the place she brought in an expert on feng shui, who warned her against certain corners, and the whole house filled with plants, clay jars to trap the negative energy, twenty wind chimes, dream catchers around the beds, and seven little fountains. Three thousand dollars I laid out for those fountains, which spread seven soothing gurgling sounds throughout the house. The expert also advised us to put all kinds of plants on the porch, mainly tree wormwood, rue, mint, and lavender.

"And you know when Mandy—may they forgive her up there—ordered the movers to bring the containers from the old house in Neve Avivim?"

"When?" asked Bahat in a bored tone.

"The eve of Rosh Hashanah! So she'd have time to arrange everything without losing working days. That year the holiday went on for four-and-a-half days. I thought I'd go crazy with her timing. She wanted me to take part in the excitement of unloading the boxes and arranging the things. I told her she could manage on her own and went to stay with a friend of mine who lives in a seventy-year-old house in the center of Tel Aviv. On the first day, Mandy rang me on my cell phone, and sent me text messages as well, to come and help her. I didn't answer. On the second day she stopped trying to contact me. She could understand me."

"And now she's dead," said Bahat and almost felt sad, as if she knew her.

"Dead isn't the word," said Gruber, suddenly seeing it in a new light.

"Tell me," continued Bahat, who noticed the change in his tone, "don't you miss your children?"

"Of course I miss them," he said.

TWENTY MINUTES LATER, when she managed to get away from Gruber for a minute, Bahat phoned Professor Raffi Propheta.

"What I suggest," said Propheta to his friend on the American East Coast, "is to find him a hotel in Neve Avivim through the Internet, it's out of season now, there must be a lot of offers. The main thing is for him to go back to Israel."

"I can't take any more, Raffi, I'm on the verge of a nervous breakdown myself. I have to start preparing my speech for the twentieth of next month, and instead of that I spend the whole day preparing his food," she said and sat down in an armchair.

She concluded the conversation and said to Gruber through the closed door of his room, in other words, her room, "I'm going to sleep, I'm worn out. Forgive me. If you want to eat you'll have to heat something up in the micro-wave. You can take a frankfurter and fries out of the freezer and put them in for five seconds. Whatever it says on the packet."

And then she shut herself up for three hours in the guest room of her house.

WHEN SHE RECOVERED her strength the world was a differ-ent place. Gruber was starting to make a little more sense. Perhaps it was the light at the end of the tunnel, or perhaps it was only the putrefaction reflecting the light of a glowworm.

"What I'm going to do when I get back to Israel," he said, "is to try to get rid of the apartment. You'll see how many people will jump at it. I can sell it at an exorbitant price because the neighborhood is very much in demand. You can always find a millionaire couple with a villa in the original Tel Baruch, or in Afeka, who want their son or daughter to live in Tel Baruch North, next to them. People are very keen on the place for their offspring." Suddenly his face clouded over. "I hope that the two years we lived there didn't affect the value of the property."

"No chance," said Bahat confidently. In her childhood in green Ramat Aviv she had often heard the weighty phrase "the value of the property".

"I don't care if I lose money," said Gruber decisively, in an animated tone.

"I'm not prepared to go back to that rootless place. Sometimes I actually feel that I don't exist there. I wonder if we have a psychiatrist in the neighborhood, and what he thinks of it. It really is interesting—is there a psychiatrist who actually receives clients in the neighborhood?"

"Of course there is," said Bahat.

Gruber poured himself glass of cider, drank it and went on:

"It's very clear to me now. Mandy helped me a lot with the trauma of moving house, and her death released the trauma from its latency."

Gruber's nagging wore Bahat out to such an extent that she forgot the positive feelings she had begun to feel toward him ever since he called her "my dear."

THERE WAS A LONG SILENCE which lasted until Bahat said, "So what now?"

"I have to go back to Israel. To carry on with the project. To carry on with life."

"Oho!" cried Bahat, but the cry contained a measure of regret, since she had already grown accustomed to this character, and now she would return to her loneliness. But not for long, she encouraged herself, only until the twentieth of next month, and then into the field, to mingle, to laugh, to eat, drink, and be merry with people of her own age.

And this weekend the girls were coming. It would be a lot more convenient for her to receive them without him.

"The chain must continue, and the watch is not yet over!" he declared.

"Of course the watch isn't over yet and the chain isn't finished! You're still before the peak. After you complete the T-suit you'll be famous, I will read about you and what you've achieved in your life, and I will tip my hat to you. You could still get the Nobel Prize. You deserve it now. Are you so abnormal that you would turn your back on that?" Bahat was already smiling.

THE TWO OF THEM spent the last night in the same bed, in Bahat's original room. Both of them shared the view that life was short, and the fact that they wouldn't see each other again ignited a great and passing lust between them.

In the first half of the night they talked and became very close. Irad told Bahat about embarrassing scenes he had had with executives from Singpore, Thailand, India, China, and Japan, due to differences in mentality between the Levant and the Far East. The woman from Ithaca split her sides laughing. It was a long time since she had laughed so much. She leaned on his flabby white chest, and hung on his every word like a child listening to faraway fairy tales.

At one o'clock in the morning he said that he had to sleep, he had a flight to New York in the morning. She ordered a wake-up call for four in the morning, but she hardly slept. At five o'clock they set out for the friendly little local airport. On the way there McPhee said to Gruber that if for any reason Tel Baruch North upset him, he should go to a hotel in Neve Avivim.

"There isn't a hotel in Neve Avivim," he said.

"Then go to some other hotel. You're so sensitive, and you've been through experiences that in my opinion demand rehabilitation. A remedial experience, perhaps."

He told her not to worry, and at the terminal he also thanked her for everything, but everything, including her sympathetic attitude toward his crisis, and *of course* for handing over the important information, and added that he hoped he hadn't gotten on her nerves too much with his demanding presence.

He shook her hand with a warmth she hadn't encountered for years, to such an extent that she thought that perhaps he had a fever, and that all his behavior since hearing about Mandy's death was the result of some virus. Gruber turned away to go through the security check, but stopped and turned round.

"Can I ask you a personal question?"

"What?" she looked exhausted.

"Why did you really give away your research? You could get the Nobel Prize for it yourself."

She was relieved that this was the question, and she replied:

"That's exactly what I feared. I felt that I was on my way to a Nobel, and I didn't want to go on. I'm not built for the Nobel, I want ordinary friends, not admirers. Do you understand me?"

"I understand you very well," he said, and she tried not to let him see her farewell tears.

He waved to her and she waved to him, and that was it. She never saw him again.

SHE DROVE HOME and phoned Lirit and told her that her father was on a plane to New York, and that she hoped he would reach home safely. Perhaps she should find him temporary accommodation in Neve Avivim, or in Tel Aviv. He had a mental problem with returning to their new neighborhood.

Lirit wrote down the numbers of her father's two flights to New York and Israel, and thanked Bahat for all she had done.

After she put the phone down Bahat drank the half can of Coca-Cola left in the house from Gruber's visit and got rid of a few prominent signs of his presence, although it was clear to her that a more thorough cleaning would be required. She stripped the sheets from the double bed on which they had let themselves go a little wild the night before, dropped them into the laundry basket, threw a clean sheet onto the bed, took off her clothes without any strength and dropped them on the floor, put on an old flannel nightgown, and got into bed. In spite of the superficial cleaning she had done, Gruber's smell was still in the room, and she got up and drizzled geranium oil in all the corners, and indeed the pleasant scent absorbed Gruber's smell and she could forget him.